RAVEN'S CRY

A story by

Jane E. Corton

DEDICATION

This book is dedicated to all those who have unfinished stories waiting to be told.

CONTENTS

CHAPTER ONE 1

CHAPTER TWO...9

CHAPTER THREE...13

CHAPTER FOUR...19

CHAPTER FIVE...22

CHAPTER SIX 27

CHAPTER SEVEN 31

CHAPTER EIGHT..36

CHAPTER NINE..40

CHAPTER TEN 47

CHAPTER ELEVEN 53

CHAPTER TWELVE..64

CHAPTER THIRTEEN 67

CHAPTER FOURTEEN..71

CHAPTER FIFTEEN 75

CHAPTER SIXTEEN..82

CHAPTER SEVENTEEN 87

CHAPTER EIGHTEEN 97

CHAPTER NINETEEN 105

CHAPTER TWENTY... 108

CHAPTER TWENTY-ONE 113

CHAPTER TWENTY-TWO 120

CHAPTER TWENTY-THREE 124

CHAPTER TWENTY-FOUR 128

CHAPTER TWENTY-FIVE.. 131

CHAPTER TWENTY-SIX 134

CHAPTER TWENTY-SEVEN.. 136

CHAPTER TWENTY-EIGHT... 138

CHAPTER TWENTY-NINE... 143

CHAPTER THIRTY.. 146

CHAPTER THIRTY-ONE.. 149

CHAPTER THIRTY-TWO.. 151

CHAPTER THIRTY-THREE.. 155

CHAPTER THIRTY-FOUR.. 159

CHAPTER THIRTY-FIVE.. 162

CHAPTER THIRTY-SIX.. 165

CHAPTER THIRTY-SEVEN 167

CHAPTER THIRTY-EIGHT... 168

CHAPTER THIRTY-NINE 169

CHAPTER FORTY 170

CHAPTER FORTY-ONE.. 172

CHAPTER FORTY-TWO 174

CHAPTER FORTY-THREE.. 175

CHAPTER FORTY-FOUR.. 176

CHAPTER FORTY-FIVE.. 177

CHAPTER FORTY-SIX.. 178

CHAPTER FORTY-SEVEN 180

CHAPTER FORTY-EIGHT 181

CHAPTER FORTY-NINE 184

CHAPTER FIFTY.. 186

CHAPTER FIFTY-ONE.. 189

CHAPTER FIFTY-TWO... 192

CHAPTER FIFTY-THREE.. 196

CHAPTER FIFTY-FOUR... 199

CHAPTER FIFTY-FIVE 201
CHAPTER FIFTY-SIX 203
CHAPTER FIFTY-SEVEN 205
CHAPTER FIFTY-EIGHT 206
CHAPTER FIFTY-NINE 207
CHAPTER SIXTY 209
CHAPTER SIXTY-ONE 212
CHAPTER SIXTY-TWO 214
CHAPTER SIXTY-THREE 217
CHAPTER SIXTY-FOUR 220
EPILOGUE 221
ABOUT THE AUTHOR 222

ACKNOWLEDGMENTS

Many thanks to my daughter-in-law, Bee Barff, for the perfect illustration to go with my story, and to my daughter, India Rabey of The Way Design, for creating the perfect front cover.

CHAPTER ONE

There was a path there and there were ravens in the mist. The sea murmured beyond the trees drawing me forward to a long, grey shoreline. The sea was quite still and silent but for the susurration of wave on pebble. The sound stilled me as I looked northward but there was no distant sail gleaming on the bright horizon. The call in my heart was not answered and as I felt the familiar ache once more, the sea and the sky parted to reveal the silver disc of a winter sun. With eyes smarting from the light or from the pain I turned away.

Following the path back, the path that only I knew, through the trees which hemmed the village round, I thought again of that day now so long ago. That day when we parted, seemingly forever. There was such desolation and a longing in me that raising my eyes to the sky, I cried out. The ravens hearing fell tumbling from the trees, mocking my cry with theirs. And there was no peace. There never had been any peace since that day.

I remember your hands that day so well, how they stroked my hair and how you said that light was for ever caught in its depths. I remember how, as my hair fell over my shoulders your hands lifted it and your fingers reached through its softness to cradle my head and your face was buried there and your lips were on my neck and my throat and I felt something deep within me answer the insistence of your breath in my ear. My head turned and for a moment we held each other's gaze, then letting our breath go as one our mouths met for the first time and the shock of it was as that of diving into a glacial sea and I thought I should die of it.

You picked me up and holding me tightly carried me away through the trees and out of the blinding sunlight, putting me down finally. Smoothing the hair from my eyes and my face, you kissed each place your hand had touched until I thought that I should have to wait forever for your mouth to find mine again and the waiting was an agony.

And then there you were, stealing the breath from

my body with your kisses and I lay in your arms as my whole being was centred on where we touched.

There on the grass my body felt as taut as the strings of the harp though the song we played was for no ears but our own. Each touch was a different sound in my head echoed by you, responding and vibrating in time and in tune. And there in the silence of the trees and the beauty of the summer, you took me, lovingly, gently, for the first time. And little did we but know – the last time for a lifetime.

For we lived in sad times. Times of uncertainty and death.

When we returned to the village my father was waiting. Though he said nothing then, he knew and I was fearful but he was taken up with other more urgent business.

Everywhere was in turmoil and you were called to fight. The men from the north, in their great ships not so unlike our own, had sailed out of the mists and fogs of the northern seas. My father was powerful and could call upon many men to defend our land.

Without a backward glance at me, shaking and trembling with fear for you, you tightened your sword belt and leapt forward into the teeming mass of men and dogs and danger.

My father's horse was led out into the sunlight, snorting and anxious and children scurried out of the way of its huge feet. Mounted, my father seemed huge and distant. You stood at his stirrup, shining and eager and you had no thought for me. I turned away running into the gloom and peace of our hall, to find my mother hurriedly putting provisions into a leather bag for my father.

Not seeing me there she rushed out and thrust the bag into my father's hands. For a moment he held her hand and smiled, just for her alone and for them fleetingly, no-one else existed. Then the horse pulled away and fastening the bag down my father called to the men behind him and suddenly there was a hush as everyone found their place. The women stood back, some clutching babies and some holding their small ones out of harm's way, but I could only stand in the doorway, in the shadows where I could not be seen. Furious with you for your seeming indifference, your forgetfulness about what had passed between us, not thinking of what you might have to face this day. I turned away angrily when I saw you searching for me and I would not watch you go.

I could hear the shuffling of feet on soft earth as my father and his fyrd of freemen left the village. There was silence broken only by the mewling of infants and babes as the women watched their men go each one wondering, would he return.

And I – dashing tears from my eyes flung myself on my sleeping furs and wept as if I should never cease from weeping but from fear or anger I neither knew nor cared.

When I awoke it was dark and as I looked about the hall it appeared strange that there was no noise, no shouting or arguing and then of course, I remembered. I did not weep but gazed around me, seeing in my mind's eye the dark head at the fire bending over the strings of the harp, plucking from it hauntingly beautiful sounds. And now those long, gentle fingers were clasped tightly round the sword just recently forged and sharpened for him and I shuddered, casting the image from my head, determined to forget about him. And yet, I prayed he should not die nor come to any harm at all, and was sorry for my childish anger.

I went over to the fire though the evening was warm and I did not need its warmth. My mother was stirring something in a pot and I stood close to her. She put an arm around me but did not break the rhythm of her stirring. We stood together she and I without speaking. There was no need for words between us. Often she knew what was in my heart without me having to voice what was there.

A log broke in the fire and collapsed into sparks and splinters which made us both start at the noise and laughing finally we moved apart. I reached for more wood and piled it on high making the flames fly upward, perilously close to the thatch and threatening to set alight the ancient beams. One of the old men, I think he had been friend to my father's father, hobbled up dragging his useless leg behind him as best he could in his haste and muttering, raked the fire down and returned to his place where he sat mending harness thus ensuring his place at the hearth of his Lord, while those who were able went to the fight. I watched his face and saw there all the anger and frustration that a warrior must feel when he can no longer do that which once he was trained to do and in which he exulted. Feeling compassion for him I poured out a measure of the honey-drink and took it to him. Pulling hard on a thread, he nodded, thanking me, then bent to his task once more.

Idly I watched the evening business of the hall. The women scolding the children to quiet and sleep. The old men pushing benches out of corners and pulling their furs out from where they had been stowed that morning. Ashes were thrown on the fire and smoke momentarily billowed heavenwards and my eyes followed. I could see stars through the smoke-hole which were then obscured by smoke and I saw nothing saving my own fears.

I slept that night deeply as one who has no fears, and awoke to a peaceful morning refreshed and at ease. The hall was still and quiet though the fire had been started into life once again and pots had been put to boil and bubble. Taking stock, I stared round and saw my mother's place empty already and finally I bestirred myself knowing that there was always much to do and I would be needed.

I went out into the morning, my eyes drawn automatically to the way through the woods where you had passed yesterday but there was no sign, no warning that you might be returning so I turned away once more.

The sun was bright, lifting people's spirits as they read into the weather omens of promise and encouragement. I, though, required more than this to lift my spirits and make my heart glad.

I found my mother with the milk-cows putting pails of the frothy, warm milk to one side where they could not be accidentally spilled. At this time of year when all things were there in abundance we had to set stores by for the winter months and there were cheeses to be made. Great round, warm, yellow cheese eaten in the depths of winter to remind us of sunshine and plenty. And so, my mother was careful not to let any drop spill as she dealt with the cows and the number of pails grew apace until at last she stood straight and had finished. Seeing me, she rubbed her hands on her kirtle and taking both mine in hers, warm and soft from their exertions, she smiled and we returned together to eat.

We were the last to the meal and had to scrape the pots to fill our bowls then sitting in companionable silence near the doorway to catch the breezes coming off the sea we watched the ravens wheeling up in the blue unconcerned with what went on below them. *How lucky they are,* I thought but said nothing out loud. Our thoughts are known to none, not even that day to my mother and perhaps not even known clearly to myself. Not then.

CHAPTER TWO

As the day drew to its close and still there was no sign of my father nor any of his men I became aware of a growing unease in the village.

Children were fretful and impatiently hushed. Tempers were short and dogs fought on the midden over week-old bones.

And the ravens were gone.

I looked up into the trees at the edge of the village, through the great canopy of leaves that trembled in the evening breeze and there was no sight of them. I remember thinking it strange that they had all left at a time when they were used to settle in their roosts.

And then I smelt it. Others in the settlement lifted their heads and the dogs, hackles raised, looked to the forest's edge and my gaze was dragged unwillingly in that direction also. We could see a darkening of the light but it was an unnatural dark. Everyone left their home and tasks to look and listen and my mother, ashen-faced, rushed to the wicket and stood there shading her eyes from the evening sun and straining to see what might be there. The smell of smoke hung in the air, faint but unmistakable and then was cleared by a sudden gust of wind blowing from the sea but our heads and our hearts could not clear and there was no sound coming from the still figures all gazing westward.

Then we heard it.

When the wind had changed direction as it often did at that time it brought to our ears the sound of men in flight.

My mother was the first to move. Looking wildly round, unseeing eyes distended with fear and the dawning realisation of what must have taken place beyond the forest, she saw me and dragged me unresisting with her. Taking command of herself and everyone else, shouting orders and instruction, scattering poultry and dogs which set up a fearful barking, she pushed me into the hall.

The old man, the mender of harness, was standing tall and as straight as his age and disability would allow clutching with a firm hand, his aged and venerable sword. I skidded to a halt breathing deeply and unsteadily as he motioned me to get out of the way and hide myself. But where to go? I looked around me desperately. My mother too was searching, casting about with eyes bright and clear and then it seemed as if we both had the same thought at the same moment. We should hide ourselves in the rubbish pits.

Grabbing furs under which we could shelter we raced out of the hall along the side of the channel which trickled through the village towards the sea. All about us there were women and old men rushing and children screaming. I fleetingly glimpsed one old man hastily digging down into the soft earth and thrusting into it a leather purse as his anxious family bade him hurry.

The village was being left deserted as people tried in desperation to save themselves from the fury and carnage that should surely catch up with us all. And we, my mother and I were not running away but trying to find safety where we were. I was suddenly frozen with fear.

'We too should run away!' I wanted to scream but my mother would not let me be and slapped my face to bring me to my senses and with great, gasping sobs, I followed her into the slime and filth of the rubbish pits.

We neither of us cared about the stench in our nostrils for we could smell only our own fear which clung about us and seeped into our very souls. Crouching beneath the furs we stilled ourselves and waited. All about us the silence grew, broken by the plaintive mooing of cows left to wander at will. Even the dogs were gone.

Then we waited.

CHAPTER THREE

We lay, my mother and I, for what was an age among the rubbish, hardly daring to breathe and without moving.

With all other senses denied us our hearing became sharper and each sound we picked up was loud and close and we had to stop ourselves from crying out when we heard men crashing through the trees.

We knew that my father was lost. And all the men with him. All the men? My breath caught in my throat as I thought this. I would never see him again. Never see again that gentle face which was now dearer to me than any. And my soul cried out as part of me died there but I could not grieve, not yet. There would be time for that later – if I lived.

Clamour was all about us as homes were ransacked and I could hear fighting in the hall which ended with a great roar. The harness mender!

He had died as a warrior should and I was glad for him but how foolishly brave he had been.

There were voices above us. The strange guttural voices of the Northmen floated in the air above our heads as they searched in their rage for more of our Saxon souls to be set free.

Some went away into the trees to find what or whom they might find there.

It was quiet at last and not heeding my mother's warning hand I looked from beneath the fur and gasped, caught unawares by the sight that met my startled eyes. The most enormous man I had ever seen was standing close to the edge of our hiding place. It was our good fortune that his back was turned from us as he stared seaward for surely he would have seen my face, white and stricken as it must have been under the shadow of the fur. In that short moment his image was for ever etched on the mirror of my memory. I noted every detail, from the shining helmet, dented on one side, flattening down a mass of unruly red hair which sprang from beneath its iron rim and tumbled down his back in an unruly sprawl, to the pommel of his sword. This sword was a wonder and would have demanded the strength of two men to heft it so great was it. Yet this one man carelessly held it loosely in his left hand and it caused him no concern.

I wondered then, was he one of the berserkers of whom I had heard tell? And yet he was quiet enough and still enough, now. There seemed to be no echo of the battle fury upon him and though his sword was smeared with red, his clothes remained unbloodied.

I felt rather than saw him stiffen as he became aware of movement behind him. I crouched in an agony of terror lest he look beneath his feet and see me there. And then I saw him bend over about to root through the mess and find me there. I froze. At that moment, my gentle, selfless mother acted and springing up, flung the fur from her and over me. Thus, was I saved. As she moved she pressed me down and I knew that I was not to follow and must stay hidden, no matter what.

The red-haired giant lurched backwards taken by surprise and he let out a yell. Making the most of her temporary advantage, my mother ran. I could hear her feet pounding away from me. Then the unmistakable sounds of pursuit. I started breathing again, not realising that I had been holding my breath and I was light-headed and giddy, when I heard the screams.

Then I knew no more.

My senses returned slowly and I was confused and puzzled to feel myself aching all over and I did not know where I was. With returning memory came realisations that I could no longer stay here. Hearing nothing but ravens, disturbed and crying above the trees, I moved carefully under my fur covering, lifting the edge just enough so that I could see. I became aware of a hungry, tearing sound which at first I did not recognise.

Then I did.

Fire!

Looking to the trees I could see a glow creeping up towards the branches and it was this that was disturbing the birds and making them cry out in alarm. I had to move. Thrusting aside the furs I crouched low and ran.

My feet became tangled and even while I struggled to free myself, I knew.

I looked down and saw my mother, eyes wide and staring at the dark sky and the stars above us for now it was night. But she saw nothing nor ever would. Her hair was all about her and unwound and it striped the earth with gold. Her cheeks were pale and cold as I bent to kiss her though she was soft still, and I fancied I could feel her breath in the calmness here about us. Now she was gone from me and I was alone.

I closed her eyes and gently smoothed her hair around her face and laid her limbs in order as my tears fell and the fear took hold of me. I shook and could not cease from shaking as I silently bade my mother farewell. She had given her life for mine, and the Northmen, thinking no doubt that he had finally flushed out and dispatched the last of us, had left. How should I ever repay this debt that had been laid upon me? My heart was heavy and I wished too to die.

And then I realised. I had to live. I had to escape and survive. Only this would release me from the burden. Only then would her spirit rest when I had done my utmost to live. I would not die. I would live and I would love again though it would not be the same.

But nothing would ever be the same.

The world had turned.

The sun would rise and it would set. Tides would ebb and flow and the ravens would roost once more in the treetops. But I would not nor could ever settle.

How should I with all that I had loved and held dear gone from me?

And my love, where was he? How had he died? Did he think of me then, in the moment of his dying? And did his eyes see me in front of him as they clouded and grew dark? And did he call out to me?

Without looking back I raced between flames and falling embers and left the life that had been mine. It too fell in the flames and ashes and I was of a sudden some other creature. I had passed through the fire and emerged unscathed and strengthened and firm of purpose.

CHAPTER FOUR

The woman looked at the boy as he raved and tossed from side to side. He seemed to be so young to be taking arms against the Northmen. She spat into the fire remembering other times, other places they had been and she had seen their handiwork. She remembered her son.

Dipping a well-used rag into a bowl of cool water she placed it on his burning forehead. Such a long time he had lain there after collapsing at her doorway one evening. How he had managed to get there she knew not.

'The good Lord,' she crossed herself, 'has surely directed him.'

Away from the carnage and destruction that always followed a raid by these men from the north. These men with their vile gods and their ships so fast that Odin himself must be the wind in their sails. Remembering her god she made the sign against the evil eye for invoking the name of Odin. Old habits die hard.

She removed the blood-soaked cloths that covered him, cleaning him carefully and gently, counting each lived bruise beneath the dirt and the blood. His wounds were many and grievous.

He should be dead, she thought. But he clung on to what was left of his life and would not succumb to the darkness which beckoned him and drew him onwards.

She made him broth and dribbled it into his mouth and mopped it up again as he turned and vomited. Calmly and without fuss she cleaned him when he shat himself and then she covered him and let him sleep.

From time to time she would let him suck water from a clean rag. And then the fever came.

He ranted for days. About ships and ravens and a great man with hair the colour of flame and eyes of a fierce blue. She cooled him with water when he burned. His eyes sank in their sockets and she knew he was doomed. His lips drew back in a ghastly rictus but he breathed still, a rattling, choking sound that filled the air with its noise.

Waking one morning to silence she thought he had gone but no — his breathing was quiet and even. Amazed, she uncovered him to see the gentle rise and fall of his breast, thin and bony now. He was healing.

'Thanks be to God,' she breathed and began to feel tenderly towards the boy who might — almost — have been her son.

She cleaned him again and he smelled sweeter now. The stink of death had left him. Moving him gently she endeavoured to make him more comfortable. To let him sleep. He groaned in his dreaming and she thought she heard him call a name then saw a tear on his cheek which squeezed from beneath his closed eyelids. And her heart ached for his loss also, whatever it might be.

CHAPTER FIVE

The woman found him one day on a rock down by the sea. He was still very weak and was limping. He had fashioned himself a stick to help him about and this was now propped on the rock against which he rested. He was looking north out to sea. They both knew that the Northmen would not return as autumn approached and the raiding season was ended. There would be a respite for the autumn gales and the winter snows kept all raiders on shore and safe from treacherous seas. And those that were preyed upon would be safe too. To lick their wounds and rebuild that which had been destroyed. If this could be done.

The woman did not think that the boy would ever rebuild himself quite as he had been. There were many hurts to contend with, some of which could not be seen on his body. She hoped that he would tell her one day. It would help him heal. But she could not press him. She had to wait.

As she stood watching him she became aware of a change, a shift in the air about her which stretched out towards him and she felt herself lose track of time and of herself and was aware that she was being offered a glimpse of something beyond her reach. This had happened before – once. And her son had died because he did not heed her words. Would this one listen? Would he hear the words that she shouted now into the wind? Startled, he turned at the sound of her voice and was alarmed to see her so rigid, so still.

She could see him etched clearly against a background of shifting shapes. He was unmoving. As she looked the shapes took solid form. She saw a girl. She changed, unsmiling, into a beautiful woman. There was a husband, but there were no babies. The husband grew careless and uncaring. The woman was sad and hopeless. The images faded.

Then beneath the thin, wasted figure on the rock appeared a huge Northman in a shining helm. He had flaming hair and it blew around him. His head was thrown back and he was laughing.

The scene changed. She saw the boy, now grown to manhood, proud and strong and wielding a sword.

He fought in the shadow of a great building on a cliff high above a grey sea. There was a light about his head and he was shining and fierce. None could withstand him. And on his shield was a raven and in the sky above appeared the god Odin with hands spread over the warrior. She knew then that he would become one of Odin's own.

As she became weary she saw the warrior with the woman and they were lovers. She smiled for the peace and delight about them was a physical thing that she could feel. Then suddenly it was gone and she saw the woman plead with the man who listened not and turned again northward.

And last of all she saw his body and the shattered remains of the raven beside him – and yet...

She could no longer speak, was deathly tired. She could not tell him of those final scenes, could not warn him, and she shivered with a cold that she had never felt before. Her teeth rattled in her head and she fell in a dead faint.

For a moment the boy did not move, too surprised at what he had just heard. Forgetting in his haste his stick he hurried over to her side. Her eyes were showing white and her breathing was coming in great, ragged gasps. Dropping painfully to his knees he clasped her frozen hands, rubbing the life back into them, and was relieved to see her fluttering eyelids indicate a return to life. She breathed deeply again and opened her eyes. He helped her sit up and she wept as if her heart would break and life was no longer worth the effort. She tried to tell him of her final vision but her tongue cleaved to the roof of her mouth and she was not able.

As the sun moved through the heavens the boy held the woman in his arms rocking her gently, giving back to her the comfort and care that she had lavished on him. She held on to him as if she was drowning and he was her only lifeline. And thus they sat each lost in their own thoughts and the day wore on until an encroaching chill made them shiver.

Leaving the woman, the boy returned to the rock for his stick, thoughts racing in his head taking him nowhere. Turning back to her he was struck by how frail she seemed. As if his returning strength was at her expense and he vowed to stay with her for a while. She deserved this consideration. His life would wait yet awhile and he knew that he needed rest.

Together they retraced their steps through the trees to the clamouring of hens waiting to be fed and a cow needing attention. It had been a strange day.

The two were silent in their tiredness and slept early, a deep and dreamless sleep as the autumn gales whipped through the tops of the trees.

And the ravens cried.

CHAPTER SIX

It seems now that the time I spent stumbling through the woods was of many days' length though then it seemed but a short time. The sun rose and the sun set and I stayed in the trees, hidden and still as the wild things were. I became one of them. I watched people pass by close to me and they knew not that they were watched.

The leaves of summer turned to the gold and red of autumn. They fell in my hair and stayed lodged there. My face and hands were stained with the juice of berries. I felt that I was becoming part of the forest and invisible. I became braver.

As I watched each day secretly from beneath the trees I saw the same man leave his village. He was tall and dark-haired. This made me sad for some reason though I knew not why. One day as he passed by me he stooped quickly down, leaving bread and cheese there on the grass and went on his way.

I stood gazing at the offering that lay there. And I remembered the taste of cheese in my mouth and like some wary animal, I darted out a hand and picking up both bread and cheese I raced back into the shadows. I fell on the bread, tearing it into great chunks which I stuffed into my mouth only to fall retching on the ground.

At last my body quieted and I knew that tears were coursing down my cheeks in ceaseless torrents and I heard my cries and was startled by the sound of a voice that I had not heard for many weeks. It was cracked and harsh. The voice of an old woman.

Who was I?

And dimly the memories started to return.

Carefully now, I broke the cheese into small pieces and chewed each mouthful slowly before swallowing. It tasted good and helped my mind to come back to me.

I noticed everything about me as if for the first time. My clothes were rags. My hands and feet were scratched and scarred. The nails were broken and black. My bones stuck out which once had been covered with soft flesh. I cried afresh and wondered where I had been for so long and how I had survived and been safe when all around had been fighting, terror and the Northmen. I shivered at that particular memory. Of that particular memory. Of that particular Northman. He who had killed my mother. How had he not found me?

I was thankful then.

I slept that night, exhausted and unafraid at last.

In the morning I tried hard to cover myself with my rags. I scrubbed at my face and hands with the first, frosty, cold water of autumn and dragged bony fingers through the tangled mass of hair that hung down over my shoulders. I was unable to braid it but tied it back with strands of ivy. I could not realise then what a fearsome sight I presented but felt better and less strange.

I looked at the place that had been my home – my lair – and saw it clearly. It was an earth cave under a great mossy oak and well-hidden. It was an age-old place and must have sheltered more than me through time. I had no memory of finding it but it had kept me safe.

Now that I had awoken, I was shunned by the forest deer that had but lately taken my presence for granted. They fled at my approach where once they had not minded me. They knew I was no longer one of them. No longer of the forest. Hearing them crash away through the undergrowth, I felt that they took me with them, or at least the wild part of me that had lived there with them.

I left the forest.

I stood by the path but this time, in the light. I no longer lived in shadow.

I waited.

He came through the gate. The first to leave the village that morning. I could see him searching the edge of the trees. I moved. Stepped forward. Shaking. His head came up and he smiled. Reached out a hand. I raised my own. He came to me and I could not still the trembling of my body. He took my hands, my cold, thin, dying hands. And he held them firm. He was warm and strong. I could feel the life flow into me and with a cry – I fainted.

CHAPTER SEVEN

'Quickly! Come help me with the child!'

I picked her up as men rushed to help, leaving the cattle in the care of a small bewildered boy.

Clamouring around me, they tried to take her from me but I would not let her go now and clasped her tightly to me.

I had watched her for many weeks out of the corner of my eye. I could not remember when she had first appeared there at the forest's edge. She was so still that she seemed to be of the forest and as wild as a young deer. I had not wanted to alarm her and put her to flight so I waited. She had always been in the same place and at the same time of day.

I wondered much about whom she might be. I do not think any but I had seen her there and I told no-one.

As the summer began to fade into autumn it seemed also that she began to fade. I had to look more closely to see that she was there. I had it in my mind then that I should bring her to the village. But how to accomplish this? I thought long and hard and finally decided to lure her with food. She had obviously been surviving on the plentiful supply of foraging to be found in the forest at this time of year but it would have been long since she had tasted village food.

Having made this decision before I left for the fields yesterday my thoughts were with this wild girl. Would she return on the morrow? Or would she be frightened off never to be seen again? I hoped fervently that this would not be the case. Her fragile beauty had moved my heart in ways I had not known before.

At day's end I looked for her even though I knew that she would not be there at this time. Still I searched through the falling leaves blowing in the frosty breeze.

The evening kept my mind busy and full. The songs of the harper seemed especially sad that night as he sang of loss and of exile. One song there was that told of a woman in a forest, in an earth cave beneath an oak. Alone. And I thought I saw the girl there in his words. I hoped that she would come with me, soon.

I slept badly. My usual bed-companion held no allure for me this night. She went off in a temper seeking more welcoming arms. I watched her in the dying firelight knowing that she would not return. I wanted her no more though her swelling belly ensured that I would not be able to cast her off completely.

I lay awake throughout many of the darkest hours listening to the many noises of the hall and its occupants. It seemed a curious time, as if all were aware that something was about to happen. There were many sounds of love coming from all around me, filling my ears as if mocking my aloneness. But I smiled there in the darkness and wished them all happiness.

In the morning I was about before many of the men had stirred themselves. Elbowing my way through sleep-sodden bodies. I went outside and smelled frost on the air and winter approaching all too quickly. If she did not come she would die. The forest was cruel in winter and it seemed that this year the winter would come early. I felt a moment's panic as I thought I might lose her before she was even found.

It was still dark at this hour though the sky was lightening in the east with the promise of a fair day to come.

I went over to the enclosure where my father's cattle were penned along with those of the village. They were quite still waiting for the milking. Not for much longer would they wait thus. The milk would surely dry up as fodder became harder to find. Many of the older animals would become part of the autumn slaughtering along with the pigs and many of the sheep. And then what feasting there would be. Great, fat, blood puddings and soft tripes seethed in milk and the scent of herbs everywhere, crushed and giving off airs to mask the smells of death and slaughter. A time of plenty, surely.

I hoped that I could share this.

Leaving the animals I returned to the hall where the women were chattering and scolding children, men and dogs in equal measure.

My father came to me and we talked of the coming day. And we talked too of the Norse raiders that plagued our coast. This year our village had been spared. Others, we had heard were not so lucky and had been destroyed. I wondered then if that was where the girl had come from, from one of those villages. I thought this very possible. What had she seen? What had happened to her?

No! Not that – please, by all that's sacred – not that! And yet – it would explain much about her. I prayed fervently to the new God, omnipotent in his newness; He who had cast down the Old Ones – made sacred that which was declared profane, who was indeed powerful.

I went cold. My father asked what ailed me but how could I say? I passed over it, said that I felt Woden's birds about me. He hissed and made the sign against the evil eye then bethought himself and crossed himself instead. As the priests had taught us for so many years. But still to us this Christus was a new god. We could not yet forget those gods who had come with us from our homes across the sea.

CHAPTER EIGHT

I awoke to find myself enveloped in the softest and thickest of furs in the glow of a raging blaze. Just for a moment, a moment of intense joy, I thought myself at home at the hearth of my father with my mother close by. But then I remembered and my memories returned to rack my wasted body with great, dry sobs.

I tried to hide the sounds by burrowing under the furs. But I could not.

Strong arms lifted me and I clung to the rough cloth that rubbed against my face. My head was held firmly by a strong yet gentle hand which stroked and soothed me as my body shook and trembled.

I know not how many minutes I sat thus, my eyes swollen and bruised with tears, my crying sounding harsh to my ears until finally the noise ended. I was aware of my body drained and exhausted lying there among the tumbled furs. I fell back, my eyes already closed again, unconscious of all but the need for rest.

*

I held her while she cried, completely lost and unaware of anything but her own grief. She was as light as thistledown and her bones felt like those of a bird. I dare not hold her too tightly in case she should break. Such a fragile, delicate thing she was. Where had she held all this grief? Where did she find the energy to give vent to all this unhappiness? My heart ached for her and I wanted to protect her. To save her from further harm.

As she quieted she looked up with empty eyes which saw nothing then falling back, she slept. I gently laid her back and covered the now warm body loosely with a fur. I smoothed the tangled hair from her forehead and carefully placed a kiss on the unlined brow.

I wanted her to speak. To say one day that she loved me.

Already in such a short space of time I loved her fiercely.

Taking a last look at her I signalled one of the women over.

'Get her broth!' I said. 'And feed it to her gently so that she can swallow and become well.'

The woman went off and I left the hall.

The sun told me that it was not yet past mid-day. My conscience told me that I was late and should be working in the fields. Others were doing my work as well as their own and this was not right.

I set off walking briskly. Alone with my thoughts. My hopes. And my fears.

The woman in the hall filled a bowl with good strong broth from the iron pot over the fire. She took also an oddly-carved spoon from off the great table. Stirring the liquid she lifted spoonsful of it out which she then let fall back so it would be cool on the lips of this strange wild creature that the thane's son had brought in from the forest. She shook her head sadly as she approached the sleeping girl, noticing the pallor of her skin, the sharply angled bones which seemed to want to burst through it so tightly stretched it was. There were bright fever spots on her cheek. No – she would not live long unless the good Lord willed it.

Sitting down beside her she lifted the girl's head, scarcely rousing her from the stupor in which she slept. Oh so carefully, she dribbled a little of the healing broth into the girl's mouth. Though most of it escaped unheeded down her chin the girl took some, swallowing convulsively as she did so. And then the woman lay her back down and left her to sleep again.

This she did several times during the day, taking it upon herself also to keep away prying eyes, that the girl might not be disturbed and should have a healing peace.

And so the day passed.

CHAPTER NINE

At some time during darkness hours I was awoken by an irresistible need. I sat up and looked round. The fire was aglow on the hearth and I could see close by me a woman sitting, her head on her chest, snoring gently. Trying not to disturb her I searched for a light to take with me. I still felt tired though not so bone-weary as before and my stomach seemed to have food in it though I had no knowledge of how it had arrived there.

The woman woke with a start and seeing that I was about came to my aid. Gratefully I took her hand and followed her slowly and carefully through the sleeping hall and outside. Everything was still and quiet and much as my own home had been. This time I did not weep when I thought of my home though I knew I would again many times. We disturbed some of the dogs on our progress and they set up a barking and howling which ceased when the woman called to them. No-one stirred.

Arriving at our destination where the stream ran through the grass and down to the sea my nose was once more assailed by the reek of rubbish pits. I held the woman's hand so tightly that she cried out in pain and I was sorry. This helped me to return to my senses.

Though still weak I managed on my own to squat and relieve myself while the woman delicately turned away. Standing and readying myself for the return journey I was overcome with tiredness once more and had to be helped back into the hall and into my bed. I managed to stay awake long enough to drink some warm, savoury stuff then lay down again.

And still the hall slept on.

*

I rose early and went over to the girl. She was sleeping peacefully now, breast rising and falling gently under the covers. Her face was no longer ashen and cold to the touch.

Her eyes flew open then and she gazed unseeing and wild into my face. I moved to calm her and as I did so knowledge dawned in her eyes. Tentatively she smiled and was quiet. I thought she had a smile of such dazzling beauty that her whole face was transfigured by it.

I told her my name and she repeated it softly back to me, her voice cracked and strained. She would not be dumb and for this I silently gave thanks.

The woman came up with food and the girl ate while I looked on. She was so very thin. I felt though that she would live now, but still she would need my strength for some time yet. Of this I was certain. I would not press her for her story just yet awhile. She should speak when she was ready. Explanations could wait. I was thankful that I had saved her and that she should live. Before leaving I told the woman to bring clothes from the store and make her presentable for I knew that my father would soon want to see the girl. I trusted that he would not stand in my way of making her my wife.

*

The woman left to do his bidding returning at last with fresh clothes, fragrant with sweet herbs. She decided also that there should be a tub of steaming water and soapwort.

While she waited for the tub, the woman tried to comb out the worst of the tangles in the mass of hair and the girl sat silently trying not to flinch as each knot was summarily dealt with. She looked round her and seemed surprised that she was being ignored by all those there. The woman had to explain how the thane's son had asked that she be left alone. She heard this with relief and gratitude.

The tub was finally ready and the girl went slowly over to it. Behind a curtain the woman helped remove her rags and was horrified to see the emaciated body revealed before her. The girl flushed with shame but nonetheless was glad to be helped into the tub where she sank into the steaming fragrance and felt the dirt and despair of the past weeks dissolve in the soothing water. She closed her eyes.

*

As I lay in the water, relaxed against the side of the big wooden tub, I closed my eyes and breathed deeply, inhaling the scents of summer herbs and flowers, and was refreshed. I put my head in the water and between us the old woman and I cleaned and washed my hair. We found leaves and twigs and all manner of things there and I was able to smile. I felt better.

Dressing in fresh clothes again was wonderful and I revelled in the softness of the cloth against my skin.

There must be skilled weavers here. I looked forward to meeting them and surprised myself with this thought. Was I then going to stay here? How would I stay here? What would or could I do? My mind became confused again and I decided that I would think about this later – not now. There was no need yet. I must become completely well. I must rest. I must build up my strength.

We brushed out my hair, the woman and I, and she gave me a sliver of shiny copper so that I might see the result. This glittering piece of metal was a precious thing, the likes of which I had not seen before, decorated with swirls and fanciful creatures. So enamoured of this thing was I, that the old woman had to remind me to turn it over and laughing I looked at myself and was astonished. My hair gleamed and my eyes burned bright in their sockets and my lips were red once more and full, not drawn tight against my teeth. I yawned then, a great involuntarily movement making me realise how unwell I still was.

I lay down on my bed again and slept.

*

That evening I returned to the hall knowing that I would have to speak to my father, to say something about this girl from the forest. I was nervous and wished that my mother were still with us. My father was not always a reasonable man and I had no wish to fight with him. The times in which we lived were troubling enough.

I went over to the girl who was sleeping again but what a transformation. I was so pleased with how she looked now and could not wait to speak with her again, though the old woman cautioned quiet. I agreed to wait until she should awake naturally and peacefully, and without alarm.

I ate then. It had been a long day and the food was good. My friends and companions glad to see me amongst them once more, talked loudly and when the harp came round made me take it up and sing.

I sang a lay of Beowulf and mention of Sigemund amongst its verses, slayer of dragons, caused some to bang tables in acknowledgement of his bravery and glory. It served to remind all there that we too had our history, our pride and should stand against the raiders from the North when they came again as surely they would. As the song ended there was a silence then feet were stamped and voices were raised in appreciation as I passed on the harp.

I turned to go outside and came upon the girl standing close by me. I could scarce breathe as I took her hand and said her name to those sitting there.

My father beckoned us over and I led her to him. He was kind to her and did not press her for information she might be unwilling to give.

'I thank you and everyone here for the care I have received,' she said quietly. 'And I hope that I might find a place here to stay and live.'

'You are welcome, my child, now go and eat and find your place.'

My father indicated that he wished to speak further with me and I watched her go to sit with the old woman.

CHAPTER TEN

We decided, my father and I, that we should try as gently as possible to find out something of the girl's story. He knew I wished to marry her and as yet said only that we should know more about her. As I was his only son I had responsibilities that should make me wary and this I promised.

The days passed and the girl grew in strength and loveliness. I spent as much time with her as I could. Gradually she involved herself with the daily life of the hall and found a place for herself. She proved to be a weaver of some ability and could often be found quietly absorbed in her work at the looms at the back of the hall. She felt happy, she said. She was able to repay my kindness to her in some small way. I had to assure her that we were grateful to her for the lovely work she was doing. And she smiled. A rare thing for she did not often smile. I stored away these moments in my memory and would think of her when I was away from her.

We were busy then for it was time for the winter kill. The days were long and exhausting and everyone had some part to play. The girl took it upon herself to wash and clean gut so that it might be dried and used to sew up hides and felt. The women found her help useful and were pleased although they regarded her with unease still. Occasionally I would catch one of them making signs against the evil eye when her shadow fell upon them. I thought them foolish and assigned it no importance.

Eventually after many days' work all the meat was dried, salted or set to cure in the beams above the fire. The Bloodmonth was over.

Yule was upon us – the midwinter – and still I had not spoken to the girl. I thought that now might be the time when all was merry with feasting and stories and we were safe and warm while winter raged about us.

It had been a hard month and the work though welcome was tedious. It helped me to cease from thinking and wondering. My saviour was constantly about me when in the hall, smiling and caring. I basked in the warmth of his attentions and was consoled.

Though I still felt not quite at home. The other women did not accept me always and I was sometimes excluded from their company. I knew not if or how I had offended but stayed friendly if I could.

There was one in particular perhaps a little older than myself and heavy with child, who seemed to take special delight in spiteful things. She it was who caused the loss of a great part of the blood set aside for the puddings by causing me to be in the way of the great iron pan when it was lifted from its frame. She pushed me from behind and I fell against the thing causing it to tip and spill among the rushes.

The dogs were on the mess immediately, lapping and barking all at once and there was a great commotion. I was horrified and looked round but she was gone. I had to endure harsh glances from those who had to beat off the dogs and set the pan to rights. I felt compelled to work harder to make up for this and grew very weary.

I was glad when Yule was upon us. The work was different and enjoyable. Making honey-cakes with the precious stuff gathered long ago in the summer. A wonderful, sweet, sticky job. We laughed as we became covered in it, licking our fingers, fending off children who enjoyed this too as they tried to dip their fingers into the pots. The smallest would scream with delight if they managed to take it from under our noses. Mothers laughed indulgently and scolded them only mildly and no-one minded. The stores were full. It had been a good summer here for them. And I remembered that for us too in my home it had been a good summer – at first. I was struck with melancholy and longing.

I left the work then and went outside. There were flurries of snow in the air which was grey and cold. I looked up at the trees, leafless now and bereft of birds. As I looked, a silver sun shone through the cloud to strike my face with warm beams. I closed my eyes taking in the little warmth and suddenly felt strange. Opening my eyes in some alarm I was aware of a great silence and stillness around me. All sound was gone and I saw a solitary raven high above the trees. It came flying out of the sun and over my head. Passing over me, it gave a cry. I shaded my eyes to follow its path and I knew in that moment that he was not dead.

The knowledge hit me with such force that I cried out and fell lifeless on the ground.

I had been in the stores with my father checking the beer and mead casks when I heard her cry out. Rushing round the corner of the hall I found her slumped lifeless on the ground. Once again I had to pick her up and carry her into the warmth. I rubbed her frozen hands. Her face was deathly white and cold when I put my hand on her forehead. I reached for the beat at her throat and could feel it fluttering beneath my fingers, faintly but steadily. She would be all right.

I was strangely moved by this incident which showed me that there was still so much I did not know about the girl and that perhaps she was still not fully recovered. We should not work her so hard. I did not want to lose her.

Her eyes opened at last.

It was like some awful dream. I was back under furs looking into this man's eyes. Eyes that were cloudy with concern and worry. How should I speak to him of what passed, out there under the snow? And I knew I could not let him know that the one I truly, deeply loved was still alive. How in fact could I be so certain that what had happened was truth and not falsehood? But I did know. I was certain and my heart soared briefly only to be brought back to this reality with a jolt. I heard him ask what had happened. There was a small silence as I thought carefully on my reply.

'I think the cold air – after the heat of the fires – and I am tired.'

I turned my face from him, concealing the guilt I felt, unable to bear what I saw in those kind grey eyes. This man loved me. I needed to think. He left me warm and quiet amongst the furs. He spoke to his father and they moved away into the firelight.

The pregnant girl looked in my direction and shot me a glance of such loathing that I felt it as an assault and drew breath sharply before relaxing. I closed my eyes.

Although I did not sleep I let my mind wander where it would and I followed it through a maze and labyrinth of thought. Where was he?

The old woman came over then with a sweet-smelling draught. My nurse once again. I took it gratefully. There must have been sleeping herbs in it for very soon afterwards my eyes grew heavy.

The scheming bitch! Was it not enough that she kept my child's father from my bed? She has him haltered already. Did she really need to pull on it to bring him to her side? He who had once loved me. Who should be taking me to wife, not this mongrel bitch come in from the wildwood. Where who knew what she had been doing or how she had lived! I spit on her!

The fire hissed and flared.

CHAPTER ELEVEN

It was decided then. My father and I would go and we would find what was left of the girl's village. Yule was behind us and the winter was mild this year. An unlooked-for boon. The winters could be cold and harsh. It seemed that perhaps this year would see us all, even the animals left after the autumn slaughter, greeting the return of spring.

When I should finally marry.

She had not wanted to join us in searching for her village, being strangely silent as to her reasons. We thought, my father and I, that her memories of last summer were still painful and raw. We did not press her.

One bright, clear morning we left the village following the vague directions she had been able to give us. We rode until the sun was well past its zenith.

We stopped to rest the horses and eat.

We had passed a couple of small settlements, busy and peaceful, on our way. Now we found ourselves in a small clearing in the forest. Our talk was intermittent and desultory as we both chewed thoughtfully on our provender. The horses were cropping the dry grass nearby, stirring up the earth with impatient hooves. Looking for juicier fare than that offered by the sere stalks that straggled above the leaf carpet.

It was very calm here and we had to resist the urge to rest for too long. We did not know how far we had to go and the days were still short. Though we had planned to make camp overnight if necessary we would prefer to sleep in some friendly hall.

We removed the hobbles from the horses, leading them to a nearby stream to drink. Steam rose from their nostrils as they splashed and blew in the clear water. I wondered if this was the same stream that had served the girl when she had been living in the forest.

Without another word we continued on our way.

Eventually as the day was drawing to its close we left the trees and came out onto the shoreline. I felt now that we must be close to our destination and I was anxious though I could not have explained why.

Making our way along the winter shingle as the

waves softly rolled in, I kept my gaze fixed inland for sight of any landmarks. At last in the gloom, I could see where a stream widened out and ran over the shingle to the sea.

Shouting to my father, I spurred my horse forward. He had been dreaming, I think, for he leapt forward in such alarm that he was almost unseated. I laughed and followed.

Minutes later, we were looking over a gate at a scene of partly reconstructed desolation. This was the village. The king had obviously seen fit to repopulate it. This was Book Land I knew, as ours was, and it could not be allowed to fall into disuse.

As we stood there, a young man of some sixteen or seventeen summers came over to us. He demanded in surly, defensive tones what our business might be. We explained that we were seeking a bed for the night, being on a long journey. We said nothing of the true purpose of our journey.

His manner did not improve as he beckoned us in and showed us where we might put our horses. We spent some time cleaning the mud from their legs and rubbing them down, not wanting them to catch a chill in the winter air. Our horses were precious to us. We found fodder for them and with a final pat, picked up our things and turned.

We were immediately stopped by the sight of an ill-favoured wight heading in our direction. He hurried up and looked at us closely before speaking.

'I am chief here and the laws of hospitality compel me to find you a place at my hearth but I would hope that you will not break your journey for too long a time. As you can see we have not been here in this village for very long and there is much work yet to be done. We have little time to entertain unlooked-for guests.'

And with this he inclined his head slightly, turned and led us to a new hall in the centre of the settlement. As we walked we were made aware of hostile glances. There were no children, very few women and those few that there were, were young but graceless.

The smell of new wood assailed our nostrils as we entered behind the chief into the hall. We could see that the building was not yet completed though sound enough to keep out winter cold.

As we stepped over the rushes on the hard, earth floor I felt something close to my foot. I was about to step on it but stopped myself and looked down. I was startled to see myself reflected in the clear, black eye of a great raven. It had placed one of its feet delicately on top of mine and was regarding me with great solemnity and what appeared to be evil intent. Or that was my feeling.

I drew breath sharply and lurched back. The bird made some coarse sound then hopped off and jumped on to a stool.

'Pay him no heed. We call him Hugin. He was wounded and I was minded to nurse him back to health. In gratitude he stays with me. Strange, is it not?'

The chief moved to the bird and stroked the dark plumage thoughtfully. My father and I said nothing though we felt there was much to be said. We dropped our gear and sat, grateful for the warmth by the huge fire. The evening meal was being prepared by a small group of girls who squabbled amongst themselves and did not quite seem up to the task.

I was glad that the girl had chosen not to come with us. What was all around us would not have given her any comfort or consolation at all. There was a strange atmosphere. This was not a place in which I wished to linger.

Notwithstanding the girls' seeming inexperience, the meal we were served that night was good though the company was less than amiable. There was no harper. I raised this point with our host who sat close by us. He stopped eating and looked at us suspiciously.

'No, we are not yet completely settled here but shall be so, surely by Weedmonth.'

He paused, as if weighing up whether or not we should be privy to any more information than that. He seemed to come to some sort of decision and continued.

'As you can see this place has been only recently built up. Northern raiders there were – last summer, I think. Destroyed all here. Left no-one alive, no building undamaged.'

And yet, I thought, there was one who lived still. I made to speak but my father casually laid a hand on my arm silently urging me to say nothing. I breathed out, but thought to ask if there was a harp. I would find some lay to sing to repay the generous hospitality shown us.

Very quickly then just such an instrument was found. It made a tuneful noise as I strummed the strings and adjusted some of the pegs. I do not think it had been played for some little while.

The hall grew quieter as men ceased from eating and drank deep from their horns as they waited for my song.

What to sing? I decided upon an heroic song, 'Deor'. This tells how the scop, the poet, is a man of value and worth and thus should be treasured.

As I lifted my voice to the sweet sound of the harp I was aware of the raven, Hugin, up in the rafter looking down at me. I shivered.

'That passed away, this must also…'

The refrain rang loudly through the hall. A warning. I wanted all there to know that perhaps their time too would pass away. This land did not belong to them by right no matter that the king had doled it out to them, thinking it free. Nothing is ever certain in life. And they should know this.

As I finished the song there was a silence. Then a shuffling of feet and a squirming of bodies. All looked to their chief. He was still. A smile spread across his face.

'A good song, chief's son. If poetry and harping should be your calling then you will always find a place at my hearth.'

And then there was noise and thanks and appreciation. But the smile never reached his eyes.

My father and I drank little that night, preferring to keep clear heads. I passed on the harp but no-one wished to sing.

When we slept it seemed that we did so with one eye open.

After we had left the table many there took to drinking in earnest and voices were quickly raised in anger. Pots crashed, benches were overturned and I saw the flash of steel in the fire glow. The chief stood albeit unsteadily and shouted for peace. He looked in our direction but our faces could not be seen in the shadow.

In the morning we rose early, ate quickly and went to attend to the horses. We were brushing them when the chief found us and was strangely talkative. He told us how he had petitioned Aethulwulf himself for this land, not wanting such good land to be wasted. The king had allowed him to take possession but he had only a twelvemonth in which to make it good once again otherwise it would be forfeit.

'So you see that is why we have no more time for the finer points of hospitality. We are still making our way but we are strong and will endure. Next time you pass this way we will have a harper to soothe you.'

He laughed.

We did not like the sound, my father and I.

Thanking the man for our night's rest we walked with him through the village. He was eager to show how well they were doing and how much had been done already as if seeking our approval. We were fulsome in our praise and encouragement not wishing to antagonise this strange man.

We could not wait to leave.

We turned south not wishing to advertise our true plans.

As we left the village behind and were about to circle back a man stepped out in front of us. He was one of those who had drawn his knife last evening. We reined in the horses which stood snorting in the cold air wishing themselves to be gone.

This man spoke.

'Things here are not quite as they appear. I and others would have you know this.'

We waited uneasily for more, saying nothing and leaning forward on our horses' necks. It is always best to say nothing and listen to everything when something strange is happening.

'I can see that you are men of rank though your harper's pose was genuine enough, I warrant. The chief is indeed chief but then again – no chief.'

'What means this riddle – chief but no chief? He is either thegn or he is not. Explain yourself.'

The man merely smiled.

'I can say no more. I and my brothers are not friends of this man but for the present time we are tied to him. This is all the explanation you will have.'

He headed back to the village leaving us with a warning shout.

'Take care and make a longer journey of it if you would be sure of reaching your destination!'

He waved and was gone.

'There are things occurring here about which we know nothing, my son. I think we should heed good advice and return home in a more roundabout way.'

We left the road and struck off through the forest quickly putting as much space between us and the village as we could. After a time we heard a body of men riding at speed down the road that we had just left. We looked at each other, my father and I, and without hesitating increased our own speed and went deeper into the trees.

As the sun climbed higher in the sky we deemed it safe enough to turn north towards our own home and safety. We discussed what to do. What should we tell the girl? Should we keep from her the truth? Or only some of it?

'It is her land by right. If she wants to take it back, but I don't think she will, she should be compensated. It is good land.'

I agreed but did not think that she would want to bother the king. I thought that she would want to forget all about her life there. I would prefer this. Her life now, was with me.

This might finally be all that was needed to bring her into my arms compliant and yielding at last. My heart beat more strongly in my breast and I smiled.

My father was less sanguine.

'Careful, my son. We have yet far to go. Better keep an open mind than be disappointed.'

But I was happy.

CHAPTER TWELVE

It was noon of the third day when the travellers returned and I was glad to see them, hoping for good tidings but their faces told me that I was to be disappointed. There was a renewed emptiness in me and I felt it fill my whole being.

He came up to me and took my cold hands in his. I saw his lips moving but could hear nothing. I shook my head to clear it of the cobwebs that had filled it, in an effort to concentrate on what he was saying to me.

'And so you see, the king would have to make them pay you compensation unless you wanted to reclaim your land.'

He added wistfully, 'I did not think you would want this.'

What was he saying? Oh yes – did I want my land

back? But of course I wanted my home back, but my home was gone and could not be made whole again. My mother was dead and my father. But he was not. Was he? And his face filled my mind and I smiled.

He thought the smile was for him.

He was talking of marriage and this seemed to give him pleasure so I let him talk.

Surely he knew I could not love him, but still he wanted me. And me? What did I want? I knew well enough, but it was not to be.

I stood watching him return to his father and they spoke together, energetically, for some time. I knew they would be discussing the marriage contract, my dowry, what land I would be allowed. And I was resigned. This was to be my life now, by his side, not by the side of that other. Not now. Not ever.

I went slowly back to my work at the loom. I had introduced a new warp, a different colour from those which were the custom. I liked the pattern. It pleased me. It was a bright thread running through the dark. Like the thread of my love, running through the darkness of my life. I kept this image with me in my mind.

*

How can she ignore him like that? The wretch! He's been trying to help her and find out what happened to her village, and she, the milksop, cannot even be bothered to ask him how he is. Does he need food? A drink? A kiss?

She blushed and pressed her hand to her growing belly. She felt the child kick and smiled.

Ah well – that's better, that's life for you, growing in my body. His seed is not growing in her scrawny frame but mine which is strong and fit for a chief's child. His seed will never quicken in her flesh, not if I have anything to do with it! He's mine and I will have him back!

*

I watched the girl growing bigger by the day it now seemed, move carefully to where he stood, rubbing his head. She laid a hand on his arm and said something that made him laugh. He patted her hand as he walked off and I saw her glance slyly in my direction, distaste for me written all over her face. But why? I should ask him, I knew. Maybe I would.

Oh – the thread's snapped!

CHAPTER THIRTEEN

And then it was time for our marriage.

As I had no family left to invite or to become involved in the negotiations with my husband's family, it would be a simple thing. The old woman helped me. She found me clothes to wear so I would not look too much like a beggar. I had no gifts to give and felt very much alone. I was glad of her being at my side on the sunny morning when I would be joined to a chief's son.

I tried so hard to smile and be glad. I owed him that and he gave me many gifts, knowing I had none to offer in return.

'It matters not, wife. I have enough for both of us.'

And the priest came with his incense and his holy water and we were wed in front of the new god. The old ones were now dispossessed and adrift although there were many who still preferred the old ways and Thor's hammer still hung around the necks of many along with the cross of Christus.

The rafters rang that night with song and noise enough to waken the dead whilst I sat quietly, smiling at all around me but inside I was numb and waiting for the night to end.

And then it did.

'Come, wife, we must find our bed.'

He smiled, trying not to appear too eager but he had drunk much mead and I had not.

He took my hand and followed by his drunken companions who continued to shout and sing, we found our bed. It had been covered with fresh furs and the sheets were of the finest linen, and fragranced with herbs of rosemary and mint.

My husband pulled curtains to afford us privacy and after final shouts and laughs we were left alone.

It was very quiet as I folded my clothes and placed them in a sweet-smelling chest, a gift from my husband's father, leaving my shift to cover me. Without turning I sank into the softness of our bed and opened my arms. I would try to make him happy although I would not be.

His eyes glittered as he joined me in the marriage bed, lifting my shift and running his hand over the curves and hollows of me. I closed my eyes and gasped. It felt good to be stroked and loved again even though his was not the one my body craved.

Eager though he might be, he was careful with me and took time with his caresses and kisses and I was glad of this. Eventually he could hold himself back no longer and with a sigh he parted my legs and sank into me.

I tried not to think of the boy whose face continued to fill my mind and to concentrate on the man who was here with me now, though it was hard. I hoped it might become easier as time went on. I hoped that it would not be obvious that my mind was elsewhere. He had been so very good and kind. I would not want to hurt him.

With a great sigh he relaxed and opened his eyes, clutching me to him gently and breathing lightly in my ear.

'You are mine at last,' and I could feel him smile, 'I have waited for this moment. I had hoped that you also would feel the same but perhaps you do not. It seems as if your mind is elsewhere. Is all well with you?'

Without hesitating I answered him with caresses and soft words of my own.

'It has been a very tiring day and I am unused to being looked at and watched by everyone. I'm sorry if I have been a less than willing bedmate after all you have done for me. You deserve better and I shall be less tired next time.'

'Of course, my love. Life here is still so very strange for you and I would not press you further. All will be well – you'll see.'

And with that he turned me so I was curled against him and he slept and I was left to wonder whether or not all would indeed be well.

CHAPTER FOURTEEN

It had not been a bad winter. The boy continued to grow stronger, no longer needing the help of his stick to move around. The old woman had stores of food set by which had seen them through the worst of the cold weather. She was tidy and methodical and the hut remained warm and sweet smelling, filling the boy with gratitude for her caring of him.

As the days became brighter and the breezes held the promise of warm days the boy began to feel restless, knowing that he could no longer remain here. The old woman sensed this and though sad at the thought of losing him was glad for him that he had regained his strength and with it, his life. She put her visions to the back of her mind and hoped that this time they might prove false.

They sat one day by the sea listening to the sound of soft waves rolling over the shingle. They were silent together and the boy flung pebbles at a small rock. His aim was unerring as pebble after pebble rattled onto it. Until he stopped and turned to the old woman.

'I must leave.'

She looked on him with sadness and longing and felt that her heart might break to think of him gone. The breeze lifted his hair and she sought his eyes which were now clear and bright and the colour of the grey sea. She nodded wearily.

Each with their own thoughts gazed out to sea as if they could find answers there if only they searched hard enough.

The old woman wondered whether or not she might have sight of the future once more here at the sea's edge and she waited. But the view remained unchanging and unchanged. With a great sigh she placed her hands on her knees and raised herself up carefully and left the boy there.

He turned his face to the north feeling the wind, cold and clean with the tang of salt. He fancied that he could hear voices calling him from there but shook the sound from his head. He left this shoreline thinking never to see it again.

The day he chose to leave was fresh with the promise of early warmth to come. Having no sword, he armed himself with a great length of stout branch.

The old woman clung to him, thought of her own son and knew for certain then that this boy too would die. She could not prevent it and her heart broke as she sobbed and shook in his arms. He held her tightly, stroking and soothing her and feeling how thin the flesh which covered her frail bones. He hoped she would be all right on her own once again.

She said nothing as he left. She watched him disappear and dissolve into the trees and then he was gone and it was as if he had never been.

She was hurting and had to drag herself back into the gloom out of the sunlight which seemed to be affecting her eyes somehow. She rubbed her head, thinking that she might lay down. Only for a short while. There were still things to do. The boy might be gone, thought the old woman, but there was still the cow to be looked after. Her good companion. She smiled at the thought as she lay down and closed her eyes.

The pain seemed to grow and fill her so that she cried out. She became dimly aware then that she would die. And as the thought passed through her head it seemed to her that the pain receded and was replaced with warmth and light. Her last thoughts were of her son or the boy or were they the same? She did not know and now it did not matter because she was filled with a great peace and as she gave herself up to this welcome feeling, her heart stopped finally and she breathed no more.

If any had come upon her then they would have wondered at her smiling face and envied her, her peace.

But none came and even the ravens were still.

The cow crying with hunger broke down the flimsy hurdle which kept her close and ambled off, grazing happily into the woods.

CHAPTER FIFTEEN

As he walked between the trees the boy's head was filled with many thoughts. Yet again the girl's face came to him, tear-stained and frightened in the confusion that had preceded that terrible day. He shuddered at the memories which still returned to him waking or sleeping. He was certain she was dead. How could she not be? He lived, though it had been uncertain that he would. His gratitude to the old woman was boundless and he could never repay her for all she had done.

One day he would return and take care of her and thus the debt would be cancelled. But he was young and understood not the depredations of age. Now though he would go north, seek a life there, far from here where one life had ended.

The boy straightened his back and walked on more

purposefully. He found a well-worn path with the tracks of cattle and men about it and this he followed for it took him in the direction he wanted.

Passing close by a settlement he was tempted to enter and ask for shelter for the night but at the last moment he turned away back into the forest. From the corner of his eye he noticed an argument between a girl who was close to her time so large was she, and a tall, dark-haired man. He idly wondered what the trouble might be as he sought the forest's shelter once more.

Night drew on. It became colder and the boy wrapped his fur around him searching for a place to rest. He found a large, mossy oak sheltering, what seemed to be a cave of earth and stones. He was surprised at old signs of occupation as he settled. He slept a dreamless sleep and was one with the forest.

The morning dawned clear. The boy ate sparingly of the cheese that he had thought to bring with him and decided to strike inland away from the coast, maybe find one of the old, straight roads, legacies of an earlier invader.

It took some time to find just such a road but find it he did and he set his face and his mind, northward.

It seemed afterwards that all the days became

jumbled in his memory and he was unable to sort out one from the other whenever he thought on this journey in after times.

There were days when he saw no-one and managed as best he could catching fish in clear streams, snaring coneys or going without. Other times he could remember villages and settlements where another stout back and pair of strong arms were welcome and in return he was fed, rested and provisioned once more. There were even girls then who looked upon him with favour and desire. There was something about him, some otherworldliness that they wanted to catch hold of and keep, but he would not be stayed from his progress northwards.

One day in high summer he stood on a cliff having been drawn once again to the sea and there not so very far away was a great building which commanded a whole headland overlooking a river that drained to the sea. He knew then that this was the place seen in the old woman's vision as she mumbled and raved in her pain, and he knew that his destiny was here. His heart was pounding as he walked the last of his journey. He thought how strange it had been that he had seen no sign of the Northmen but now there was evidence of them all around. He followed the course of the river into the seething community that clustered about the foot of the cliff and the great abbey.

He saw ships – longships – everywhere. Pulled up onto the beach, onto the shingle, above the tide they lay. Some fallen and abandoned, ribs showing through rotting timbers. Others brand new, shining whitely against the mud whilst the shipwrights worked on them. Still more were being loaded with gear as others were unloaded. For a moment he was taken aback and the boy just stood there and stared, wondering where to go, what to do.

All around him he could hear the guttural talk of the Northmen as they yelled at each other going about their business, swaggering and rolling, more used to heaving decks perhaps than the stillness of the land on which they now walked.

The last time he had heard such sounds it had been to the accompaniment of clashing metal and the screams of dying men. For a moment the boy broke out in sweat that dripped frozenly down his spine. Fear paralysed him. Then his attention was drawn to a commotion centred on one particular individual. A huge man this was, with flaming hair and a great roaring laugh that was taken up by those about him, until the sound that grew from them was louder even than the most persistent of hammers that beat in the great wooden pegs of the ships.

The giant had plaited his hair into shining braids that fell heavily down his back almost to the leather belt which held both axe and sword. His head was flung back as he roared at the sky, his mirth infecting all others who came near. Even the boy felt his lips unwillingly drawn into a shadow of merriment. His face seemed unfamiliar after so long without smiling and he felt foolish. He moved up to the group and breathing deeply to still his trembling he greeted the giant with hands raised to show he meant no harm. All sound ceased as the giant turned glittering, stone cold eyes upon him.

'I wish to join with you, Northman.'

There was silence. The eyes, blue as lapis, continued to watch him. These eyes the boy was sure would miss nothing.

The giant spoke and his voice was a rumble and tumble of stones coming from deep within.

'And who are you, puny sapling? Where is the great tree that sired you, I wonder? And what makes you desire to join with the hated Northmen? For I see you are not one of us by your skinny frame, truly awful in its feebleness.'

And he laughed harshly as he moved forward and

poked the boy in his chest, knocking him to the ground.

Enraged, the boy sprang up seeming to grow in stature as he spoke.

'I am no puny sapling! And though lacking a sword such as yours am able to stand up for myself with this staff!'

And forgetting himself, he whirled and aimed a blow at the Northman's head. Before harm could be done he felt his arms grabbed and pinioned behind him cruelly crushed by many hands and his staff fell with a clatter to the ground.

There was a hush. All could hear the boy's breathing rasping out of him and tension mounted. The giant roared with unexpected amusement and the tension fell away as others joined in. The hands holding his arms relaxed and he shrugged them away, rubbing himself to ease the pain of bruised muscles.

'So the sapling has thorns, hey?'

He became more serious and dropping his head peered penetratingly into the boy's eyes. Unflinchingly the boy stared back – would not be intimidated.

'Why do you want to join us? Why would we want you? Speak!'

'I have nothing. I want to fight. With you I can

make a place for myself. Achieve glory – maybe even gold. I am young, it is true, but I am strong and unafraid and growing stronger by the day. Can you find no use for another warrior? Even though not of your blood?'

'Let me think on it.'

He turned abruptly and was gone surrounded by laughing, curious warriors.

The boy was left, his staff by his feet, cold and trembling. The first encounter had gone well. He was still alive. He allowed himself a wry smile as he retrieved the staff.

That night he slept in the shelter of one of the upturned boats and his sleep was sound and deep.

CHAPTER SIXTEEN

Early the next day the boy was shaken roughly awake.

'Follow us, boy!'

There were two men there waiting for him. They were not to be argued with. Pausing only to void his bladder he hurried after as they strode off not bothering even to look back and see whether he was following. He would have been stupid not to and he was not stupid.

The three found themselves eventually at the entrance to a forbiddingly large dwelling made of rough-hewn wood lashed tightly to withstand the northern storms. Waiting only for a signal that all was well his two guides, on receiving that signal, left him. He moved inside and realised how hungry he was as his guts churned at the sweet odours rising from the cooking pots. The red-haired giant had finished eating, his empty bowl by his shoeless feet, and he lay back against the table, eying the boy. He picked his teeth and spat in the fire, his eyes never leaving the boy's face. The flames leapt and sizzled. The boy was unmoving and stood relaxed leaning on his staff.

There was a disturbance in the rafters. He looked up. A great black raven was also eying him coldly. The boy was startled.

'That is Munin.'

The giant spoke in a companionable tone.

'He lives with me. One of Odin's birds.'

Although he spoke the boy's language slowly and with great care his words were clear and the meaning was plain. The boy appreciated the care with which he spoke. It was clear that there should be no misunderstanding between them.

'You look in need of food.'

And before he could say anything a steaming bowl was put in his hand. Tucking his staff under his arm he started to eat, burning his tongue in his haste to fill his belly. The giant laughed.

'Sit!'

He pointed to the bench beside him. Gratefully

the boy sat and spooned the thick, creamy stuff into his mouth looking neither right nor left until the bowl was clean. He felt better. He leaned back and sighed, assuming an air of ease which he did not feel.

'That was good!'

'We live well here for the land around and about is soft and fat and yielding. Not like our own country. Ah but this now —' and he banged with his horn beaker on the table, making the pots rattle, 'this is our country now. None can withstand us. My warriors are truly great. We true sons of Odin!'

He grinned wolfishly, pleased with himself. The boy said nothing but regarded the raven above him which croaked and muttered softly to itself as it preened its feathers in the smoky air.

The giant continued.

'Well, boy, I have indeed thought on it and you shall stay with us. It is true — another willing sword never goes amiss.'

'I have no sword.'

This was said quietly. A statement of fact, not complaint. Not begging nor making excuses.

'That is soon remedied. Go — and choose one from the forge. But not *too* grand, mind. You are still a puny youth. We don't want to overburden those scrawny arms!'

And with that he threw back his great head and guffawed up at the raven which squawked in alarm and flapped off to quieter parts.

'Here is where you sleep and live. There is room.'

And his hand swept the air in front of him. The boy looked around noticed the snug corners in the warm gloom. The girls and women tending fires and pots. Axes and shields hung from the walls which had been stuffed with moss and mud against the biting wind which would blow off the winter sea. He breathed deeply and the scents of the hall were clean and sweet to his nostrils. The place was well tended and cared for. He was content.

'I thank you.'

'One thing though, boy. You take my shelter and my food and you become mine.'

His eyes hardened and his face was grim as he spoke.

'These are now your people. Are you certain there is none to claim your allegiance?'

A face came then unbidden into the boy's mind, white and tearstained and his heart contracted with the pain of remembering. He pushed the vision firmly away from him. He would remember no more.

'No. There is no-one with any claim upon me. I am after this – a Northman.'

They clasped each other's arms with strong hands and laughed. The boy felt light and free. One life had ended and another was begun.

CHAPTER SEVENTEEN

It was time for the birthing. The month of Hretha and the weather was mild. Women moved around the girl trying to ease her child into the world, but it seemed reluctant and her screams were dreadful. I tried to shut out the sound from my ears, but I could not. My shuttle moved more quickly now and the warp weights clattered against each other and I could feel myself growing tense.

I left the hall and my weaving then. I could stand it no more and rushed into the forest thinking at least to search for herbs so that my time might not be wasted.

I walked for a long time in the greening forest scenting new life on the breeze which ruffled the branches above me. The herbs which I'd gathered fell from my uncaring hands as I thought on the child being born. My husband's child. I wondered then if he would return to her bed in due course, searching there for the satisfaction and release that I was unable to give him.

His love was a greedy thing and would consume him. I could not match his passion, his need of me and I knew that already he was growing resentful. He was unaccustomed to being denied his will. I could not be that which he most desired for my heart was ever elsewhere. I was sad for him, knowing that although I cared deeply it was not enough and it would not hold him. This, I knew.

The hall was strangely silent on my return.

There was not one child but two.

And although the one was fine and healthy the other was but a sickly thing and not thought long for this world. They lay wrapped and swaddled together, sleeping. The mother was resting quietly after being given a sleeping draft. I was told that the birth had been hard and then – to produce two babies! The old woman came over to me making the sign against the evil eye. Such an unlikely and unlooked-for event as the appearance of twins would mean all sorts of trouble for everyone and especially the unfortunate mother. The old woman lowered her voice and whispered hoarsely.

'No good will come of this – mark my words. No-one will be pleased by this.'

And she spat.

I laughed at such superstition. Twins were a blessing from the gods, not the curse that some thought. Or so I had thought once…

The priest came up then and blessed and baptised them in case the new delicate life in them was not up to the struggle. At least now if they did not live they would enter through the portals of Paradise. Or so it was said. Myself, I was not so sure of this Paradise and its God.

When my husband returned he went straight to the babies. The hall held its collective breath not knowing what his reaction would be. They need not have worried. He grinned hugely and picked up the bigger of the two babies who bawled lustily at thus being disturbed. This made my husband laugh and the rafters rang with the noise as everyone joined in. Except me. I looked at the tiny scrap left lying there sleeping still and ignored by all including the mother who had been disturbed by the commotion.

I picked up the little bundle gently and it mewed quietly then settled again. He did not mind the attention his brother was getting and had no objection to the noise. I rocked back and forth with him as he snuffled quietly against my shoulder. I felt at one with him in some way. He too was an outsider as I was.

That night my husband came to me already aroused and demanding. This time there were no kisses – no caresses – just hot groping hands that prised my legs apart. He sat back on his haunches and looked down at me and leaning over with both hands tore the shift from my body. His hands moved over me, through my hair and down over my breasts which he squeezed roughly, causing me to cry out. Whispering in my ear, he said, 'This night I shall fill you also with babies, my sweet. I want to see the child that will come from your body that will be a great warrior and will inherit after me. Your cries are of no consequence. Tonight you will be completely mine as you have never been before. You will give me what I desire at last!'

And with that his hands moved between my legs and inside me, urgently seeking and probing and I, I just lay letting him use me as he would. I looked at him finally seeing the fierce, burning eyes with which he gazed almost unseeing into mine. I looked down to where the hardness of him seemed almost ready to burst. I had never seen him like this and was dismayed but tried to give into him though it was not easy. There was always a part of me that was soaring elsewhere and would not be possessed.

He moved his hands and placed them under me and lifted my body from the bed. Grasping me firmly he pushed himself straight into me as far as he could. For a moment he was still then holding me tightly he moved once so much into me I thought he would never stop. I could not wriggle even to ease the discomfort I was feeling. It was as if he had almost forgotten I was there. He shuddered and his body shook convulsively as he emptied himself into me.

I thought then I might sleep and nurse my pain. But this was not to be.

Leaving my body with a deep sigh of satisfaction he grabbed my hand and made me feel him, hard still and just as urgent. He moved my hand between his legs causing me to cradle him as he continued to breathe deeply. Without warning then he turned me over and raised up my buttocks and commenced stroking and caressing me a little more gently this time for which I was grateful and I began almost to enjoy the feeling. As he kissed and stroked he moved a hand inside me again pushing my legs apart as far as he could and moving all around, slowly and sensuously, arousing me at last so that I lay quiescent and lost in the sensation. He kissed the inside of my thigh with soft kisses and tiny licks. He moved close to the hotness and wetness of me until finally he plunged his tongue into me and I cried out as he used his tongue to arouse me further. Climbing onto me, he rammed himself hard into me, ceaselessly. My body was unresisting as he moved his hands over me, stroking the hardness of my nipples, the softness of my breasts. All of me was centred on this thrusting and I felt as though I had ceased to exist. I was pure sensation. With a great shuddering cry I was released and fell forward on the bed where I lay unmoving and out of breath. I felt my husband fall beside me with a hand still between my legs. It was as if he was unwilling to let me go. Maybe he realised that with all his skill, artfully employed he had indeed possessed all of me, this one time.

I felt his fingers playing idly with me and moved myself nearer to him. For some minute I dozed and then felt him grow and harden yet again. He slipped into me very softly this time and we swayed back and forth together quietly. With a sigh he ended and lay still.

Mercifully now he slept without moving, a deep and exhausted sleep. I too slept.

I was awoken at dawn as he pushed me onto my back and took me yet again, roughly and quickly this time. It was soon finished. He said nothing and rolled off me to sleep again. I wondered how many more times I should be used thus as I watched the dawn fade and heard people moving about. I was hungry. I needed to eat and I needed to cleanse myself but when eventually I tried to rise his arm around me tightened and would not let me go. He opened his eyes.

'Not yet, my sweet. I am not done with you. There is vigour in me still. Feel me!'

Reluctantly I reached down and it was indeed true. He smiled lazily at me.

'One last time, I think!'

Swiftly, almost before I realised what was happening he had moved, caught hold of my legs and lifted them high in the air exposing me fully to his unyielding stare. He ran one finger carefully down my leg onto my thigh as he held on to one ankle. He watched this finger as it reached me and parted the folds of flesh it found there. Even now it was a delicious feeling, this tickling and stroking, and I closed my eyes to enjoy it the more. Leaving hold of my ankle he raised up my body and fastened his mouth on me hungrily sucking the very essence from my body and I groaned as I felt his tongue circle around me. Then he stopped and I opened my eyes to see him poised and ready to sink himself into me. As he did so, his movements were hard against me and I felt my very bones being jolted and shaken as he pushed deep into me, never altering the rhythm of his body's urging.

He held me still, tightly, bruising me carelessly. It seemed that he would continue on for ever, never finding the release he so frantically sought.

I was hurting now. My head was thudding. I was sore and my muscles were screaming at this unaccustomed straining.

I thought he would never stop and that I should die here with the agony of it when I felt his rhythm alter becoming yet more frenzied. His hands held my body down on him more firmly and just as I thought I could take no more with a great rending cry he held himself still inside me as the warm life of him passed from him, deep inside me.

I waited for him to let me go but instead he spoke.

'I have now possessed you truly. It will be a good strong boy that's born here this ninemonth, I think.'

And with that he gave a final thrust then left my body but holding it still as if he was unwilling to let the life flow from me. I waited, longing for rest.

We both heard the crying of babies at the same time and with a shout of glee he let me down gently.

Pulling on clothes hastily he left me to greet his sons.

I heard the crying of one baby cease. His mother must be giving suck and the other unwanted one continued his weak hungry cry. My heart went out to him. No matter how I felt I must help him. Rising from my bed, I searched for my clothes and whilst dressing I noticed the bruising on my body vivid against the white of my skin, felt the soreness between my legs and the stiffness of my muscles as I moved. I put this pain to one side thinking only of the tiny, crying baby.

I went over to the infant and picked him up. His mother looked at me but said nothing as I took him off to seek out a nurse. I knew she would not feed him indeed would want him to die but yet fearing his father's reaction if she extinguished the tiny spark of life herself. As some do with the weaklings or the damaged babies.

*

Well – what a thing! The chief's son's wife makes off with the chief's son's bastard! Let her – it will die anyway. She looks ready for the grave also, the feeble thing, with those great shadows under her eyes. My Lord's love play is more than she bargained for, I warrant. Wait until I am strong and whole again then shall I satisfy him and meet his lust with my own and I will match it. I will see that he is reluctant to return to her bed ever again.

But then he is at least here with our strong, healthy son who will make him proud. I shall see to it.

*

And with that the mother bent to stroke the favoured son's head, marvelling at the strength and ferocity of his suck as he pulled greedily on her swollen nipple. Almost she felt a thrill of lust run through her, taking her by surprise. She looked at the father standing over them both and an obscure desire clouded her eyes as she gazed at him. He was moved to stroke the breast that she held for the child taking the nipple from his mouth and seeing the milk there bent to taste it with his tongue, scandalising all present but caring not a jot for their opinion. The child at being so thwarted cried out and struggled to reclaim his place at the breast. His parents laughed together.

CHAPTER EIGHTEEN

I found a nurse for the baby in one of the homes that lay near the edge of the trees. The woman there had lost her baby shortly before the twins were born. The fine big boy had never breathed, strangled by the very thing which had sustained him for nine months. The woman was grieving. He had been her firstborn. The father was there, silent and sad also for the waste. He said nothing, leaving as soon as I entered with the infant. Saying little but with the instincts of a mother the woman took him and put him to the breast. Appearing unsure of what was expected of him at first he continued to mewl piteously. With encouragement, the wordless sounds that a mother makes to her baby, he found the milk and began to suck greedily so that the life-giving stuff trickled from his lips and down his chin. He had such a look of ecstasy on his little face that both the woman and I laughed and I knew then that he would live.

Leaving them, I returned to the hall and found food for myself noticing how ravenously hungry I was. I ached still and called for a tub to be set up so that I could soak away the night. I strewed sweet-smelling herbs in the water and the relaxing scents filled me with peace. As I entered the water and gently sat in its healing embrace I closed my eyes letting my mind ramble where it would. I thought about the baby and was glad that he was safely out of its mother's way. I did not trust her to care for it. Already I felt the ties of affection growing in me for this little boy. With a pang of alarm I wondered whether indeed there might be life growing in me also. But I thought not. I would not bring to life any seed other than that which was now denied me.

Where was he?

Tears fell from the corners of my closed eyes. How long had it been since that day when I had gladly given myself to him in the sunshine under the trees? And my heart broke once more with the pain I still felt. More sharp and hurtful than any pain my body was feeling, this anguish which would not leave me.

I called for more water and began scrubbing myself in an effort to lessen the pain and force myself to think about something else. To put to the back of my mind that which could not be altered. My tears ceased. Red and raw from the water and the scrubbing I climbed out of the tub and was enveloped in warm, dry cloths. I sat by the fire wrapped thus and let my hair be combed and dried and braided before returning to my clothes. It was good sitting there warm and comfortable by the fire and for a few moments I dozed peacefully.

The tub, still warm was offered to the girl to soothe her body. Her refusal was loud and shrill and could be heard throughout the hall.

'I shall not use that interloper's leftovers – I shall have my own water. Have I not just given birth to the son of chiefs?'

*

Her standing had changed. She was no longer a playfellow of the bed but the mother of a chief. My heart sank as I realised that now she would feel her position was unassailable and she could be more unkind and spiteful in her dealings with me. Unless I too had a son – but no, that should not be.

Her jealousy unnerved me. It was all so unnecessary.

I was willing to share my husband with her, would be happy to if it meant no more nights like the last. But her love it seemed would countenance no rival. She must be mistress in the hall. I resolved, whenever I could, to have no more dealings with her at all. I should feel safer, though I did not think she would actually go so far as to harm me. Still, I would have to look about me carefully. She had a faction in the hall which would support her against me – an outsider.

I knew that she would have been informed of the action I had taken to save her baby's life. I knew too that my husband would be told. Would he be angry? Would he insist on the child being returned to its neglectful mother? Time alone would tell.

The day drifted past and loath as I was to do anything I did return to my weaving for a short while before helping with the evening meal which was to be a celebration.

The men returned from the day's work, among them my husband who was still full of energy and tireless this particular day. He smiled at me and embraced me firmly, speaking quietly.

'You shall sleep alone tonight, my love. I will not disturb your dreams. Dream of the strong son that must already be growing in your body. Make him fine and proud for me!'

He laughed and released me. I was grateful enough to smile at him as I looked into his eyes and taken aback perhaps, he leaned over and kissed me.

The hall that night was loud and boisterous. Mead and ale were drunk in great horns that passed around the table. Dogs fought for bones between the feet of drunken men still good-natured enough to kick them gently out of the way.

I left as soon as I was able, craving the sleep denied me the night before and not wanting to witness the chaos and disorder that would surely ensue before the night was over. My husband's father was the most unruly of all, banging the table with his fists and shouting songs and snatches of poems that were meant to drive men savage with desire. Men responded with lewd gestures and grabbed girls as they passed among them with yet more ale. Those who were not able to get out of the way quickly enough were tumbled then and there among the rushes to general amusement.

I peered from behind my bed curtains and envied them not at all, although the girls were well disposed to this treatment on the whole having drunk along with the men. There was much laughter and not all of them were eager to get out of the way of grasping hands.

It was a strange night. It was as if the birth of twins had unleashed an unlooked-for power into the hall that made people less wary and careless.

I watched my husband lift the skirts of a pretty girl who leaned eagerly into his embrace reaching down to release him from the bondage of his breeches. His mouth was all over her body as she threw back her head, eyes closed, mouth open, receiving his caresses with enjoyment. I watched their coming together with detached interest. I saw him bend her over a bench and enter her from behind, hands clutching her breasts, filling his grasp to overflowing. He was cheered on by others who watched or who were themselves coupling urgently.

Finishing at last, he left her and she stood up smoothing down her skirts. She was breathing deeply and her skin was rosy in the firelight. She made no attempt to cover her breasts which rose up and down in time to her breathing as she looked round the company smiling slightly through half closed eyes. There was a smile in response as one of the young men rose and reaching over, stroked her breasts. With a quick intake of breath she turned to him and taking one of his hands drew it under her skirts where she moved it languidly up and down. Not being quite as sure of himself as my husband had been he moved into the shadows with her.

My husband laughed and looked in my direction. Ducking back I felt sure that he had seen me watching and with beating heart I anxiously awaited his response. It was not long in coming. The curtains were pulled back and his drunken, bleared eyes looked at me.

'So, little spy, you were watching me take my pleasure away from you. And how was it I wonder, watching me do to someone else what I do to you?'

He stared at me for some moments then moved towards me. I said nothing. With a gentle finger he stroked the side of my face and moving along my neck he reached the laces of my night shift. Loosening them, he pulled the shift away from my body where it lay unregarded on the floor. Wondering at his ability to feel desire again so quickly I let him stroke me, felt my nipples harden and my deepest recesses liquefy in readiness for him. Perhaps I had been aroused by what I had witnessed after all.

He took my breast in his mouth, sucking at me very gently this time. Keeping me standing he lowered his head down where he used his tongue to add to the wetness of me all the time kneading and handling my breasts softly. It was so surprisingly pleasurable all this that when he lifted me onto the bed I was completely unresisting. Standing straight, he removed his clothes and leaning over me gently slid himself into me. I parted my legs more easily to accommodate him and feel him as he moved slowly within me.

'It would seem, wife, that I am not going to let you sleep in peace this night after all. It would seem also that what is between your legs suits me really very well.'

And with that he emptied himself into me with a sigh. I was left wishing rather that it had gone on for longer so gentle had it been. He rolled off me onto the bed.

'You shall sleep now. There is yet more talk to be heard and ale to be drunk.'

He left and I lay watching the darkness. Over all the noise I could yet hear the crying of a hungry baby which soon ceased as it was attended to.

I thought on the little one in the strangers' hut and hoped that he was thriving.

CHAPTER NINETEEN

In the morning there was uproar. My husband's
father was dead. He had died where he fell, drunk and
snoring on the boards surrounded by the wreck of the
night.

There was wailing from women and lamentations.
An air of uncertainty hung over the hall. The day's
business still had to be seen to whilst we all absorbed
the changes in the circumstances that had been thrust
upon us.

The body was removed and cleaned by the women
who put him in his finest clothes, washed and curled
his hair and his beard before laying him on a hastily
improvised bier.

He had not been old and was thought to have had
years to live so his death was a great shock to us all.

I too would miss him. He had been kind to me, had ensured that the size and value of my dowry should be adequate. He would talk to me at times of my father and my home. He had made approaches to the king on my behalf to aid me in my request for compensation for my lands which had been taken over. He had helped me.

My husband came bursting into the hall and immediately took charge, calling for the priest who arrived in some confusion, not sure what should be expected of him. He was soon informed.

The burial was to be later that day in the Christian way and the old thegn would be wrapped and shrouded. There were to be no grave goods. Our land now belonged to the new god. There were some there who drew breath sharply and would have had it otherwise but knew to keep quiet. The old ways which had served us well for long ages were fading. The thegn would fill a place in the churchyard along with maybe five or six souls who were there already and his place would be marked with a simple cross. The priest would intone in a language unknown to any of us and spoken by him carelessly and with little understanding, and that should be the end of my husband's father.

My husband was dry-eyed as he watched the cold, wet earth of spring fall on his father.

But I cried.

Cried once again for the father I had lost in battle; for my mother destroyed by the red-haired giant. And also for him, who I had learnt to appreciate rather than love. Most of all, however, I cried for myself for what had gone and what must still come to pass.

I stood by my husband who placed an arm around me, pulling me close, and I was inconsolable.

The day ended finally and the hall was quiet.

CHAPTER TWENTY

The raiding season approached. The boy had worked hard proving his worth and value to these unyielding men of the north. They accepted him and knew his worth. The red-haired giant became accustomed to him. Noticed how he was always there at his elbow. He began to rely on him. To want him there whenever there were decisions that needed thought. His voice on these occasions was quiet but heard. Worth hearing.

He was no longer a boy it seemed but had assumed the mantle of manhood. It fitted him well and he was comfortable with it.

The times when he thought about the girl were becoming less frequent. Her face when he brought it to mind was sometimes unclear and he had to focus hard to see her clearly. The ache was still there but he had learned to live with it. To put it behind him, shut it out and block it off. How else could he live?

There was a girl here, daughter to the chief's sister, who looked upon him with favour, he knew. It was time to end the grieving for what was. Time to look forward. He began to seek her out in the hall at evening time. Spoke to her with care and warmth. Her responses pleased him. She was soft and pliant when at last he kissed her. Her body promised much and he felt himself disturbed by desire. Desire which for so long had laid quiescent in him. It took him by surprise but it was a feeling that he enjoyed. He hoped to feel it again soon but for the present he sought out his sleeping place and slept well even though the hall was still alive with noise and light.

He awoke to a shining day, glittering grass rimed with crystal-hard frost. The air was so still and sharp that he was sure that if there had been a breath of wind he would have a sound of tiny bells about his ears. He breathed in the pure air deeply standing by the palisade near the sea and knew now that his loyalties were to be tested. His thoughts were untroubled. His place was now with these men of the north. His life was theirs. That had been the bargain. Turning back to the hall he dismissed the face that gazed at him reproachfully from behind his eyelids, filling his mind with a clarity that took him by surprise.

Collecting what gear he needed he made his way to the boats pulled up high on the shingle out of harm's way. His spirits lifted as he saw the great raven sail of his Lord attached to the mast and rigging of the greatest of these boats. He paused a moment to take in the scene, the final moves in the elaborate game that was raiding and warfare.

Barrels were knocked over. Staves came awry, contents spewing on the ground unheeded. There were always other barrels to take their place. Always too much for too little space.

Men were hurrying, each one intent on the task in hand miraculously not stumbling or getting in each other's way.

'Like so many well-ordered ants,' he observed to himself, and smiled.

Running over the shingle he joined the throng and was aware of an urgency and excitement in the air which infected him causing his blood to race.

His great red-haired Lord was pleased to see him and clapped him about the shoulder. They moved together into the press of men.

The boy felt his scalp prickle and he looked up. He

felt eyes on him though he could not see them was only aware that they were far off and distant. The sounds about him ceased and all was quiet and stilled. He felt himself lifted out of his time and set afloat and adrift on strange seas. He caught his breath, waiting, feeling the stars whirling crazily about his head.

'She is there and she is alive!'

And he knew this with absolute certainty. And he also knew with a terrible sadness that she was far beyond his reach. He searched the darkness around him, piercing it with the fierceness of his gaze but found nothing that could help him or could answer his questions.

And then the warriors were before him again. The bustle and noise filled his head and he was back on the beach breathing heavily and sweating in the cool air. No-one noticed as he leaned against the side of the ship gathering his wits.

Where was she?

Was she still alive?

Did she think of him?

How could he know?

He was desolate and there was a gaping hole in him that nothing would ever fill.

Not even the Northgirl.

Not really…

The fleet was ready and he was glad. He leapt aboard lightly. The wooden timbers heaved and bucked beneath his feet as the ship responded to the rising tide like a woman yielding to her lover. He dismissed the vision, put it to the back of his mind. He would not think about her any more. There was no point. Things were as they were…

The offshore breeze pushed them towards a bright horizon. The sky was lightening. Dawn was not far off. He sat listening to the slapping of sail against mast and was aware of the concerted effort of will that pushed the boat onward. Oars dipped into the darkness below them. Shining blades were lifted skimming the waves whilst gleaming drops fell back into the darkness.

The ships moved onwards.

CHAPTER TWENTY-ONE

Wind and current conspired to push the boats southwards hugging the shore. The boy was aware of anxious faces peering at them from behind wattle and daub and stone alike. He could almost feel their relief as they surged onwards.

'From the fury of the Northmen, good Lord deliver us!'

And He did.

This time.

Days passed until they turned up a long grey river to a place that had seen other invaders in other times and this place had absorbed them all, changing them and being changed in turn by them.

They tied up at great long quays and went ashore into the hustle of the marketplace. Cries rang out as old friends greeted each other with jests and boasts of such absurdity that the market place was filled with booming laughter.

The boy looked round him marvelling at the displays of merchandise brought here seemingly from the four corners of the earth and even beyond.

There was amber from the Baltic, glass from the Rhineland and strange, soft, brightly covered cloth from a land where the sun rose each morning. It was said that in this land such cloth was commonplace and was worked in threads of gold and silver for the mighty to wear. The boy did not believe this. There was not enough gold in the world to buy such stuff nor goods to trade in exchange.

The boy's looks and strange darkness drew glances from young girls and women alike. He was jostled by them and felt himself flush as a breast was thrust at him by a laughing girl pushing past him with a creel of fish.

The red-haired warrior thought this a huge joke and there were many laughing at his discomfiture. He grinned also and they moved on.

The day was spent in this way pleasantly and sociably and the boy relaxed into it, enjoying himself and staying close to his Lord.

Towards evening they were joined by others who sought to end the day drinking and eating in like-minded company. The mood was easy and comfortable and stories of increasing complexity drew gasps and roars of laughter.

Then all went still and a hush fell on the crowd.

A raven trailed fearlessly behind a dishevelled traveller as he emerged into the firelight not making a sound but looking round as if to challenge any who sought to question his presence there. The boy was intrigued and watched closely as the curious procession sauntered casually up to his Lord who sat regarding them through narrowed eyes. They greeted each other carefully and with respect. The raven flapped to the stranger's shoulder.

'I see you still have the bird, twin to mine.'

His use of the other's language was well-measured and precise.

'Indeed the bird is like those of Odin, my Lord, my eyes and ears.'

And as he turned he seemed to look straight into the boy's eyes, holding his gaze. The raven too looked at him and the boy shuddered, feeling uncomfortable under this ill-starred scrutiny.

Turning back to the Lord whose gaze had followed his the stranger spoke in low tones. The boy felt the hairs on his neck rise as he strained to listen but could not.

The stranger had brought a motley crowd of hangers-on who fit uneasily into the company. There were murmurs and the mood changed. Became not ugly exactly but apprehensive, waiting.

The Lord and the strange chief, if chief he was, had their heads together and talked on, ignoring all those there.

The boy slipped away to find a place to rest. His head was still clear but he was not interested in joining others emptying horns through the night. He felt the need to be alert. He thought it's important.

He became distantly aware of growing sound – arguments – voices raised but this did not cause him to throw off his coverings, to become involved. He sank into sleep, gratefully, and knew nothing until morning woke him. He was surprisingly refreshed.

There was a new mood in the air. A mood of direction and purpose. The stranger and his bird joined the boat and sat in the prow as the vessel sped over the silvered sea.

The boy was loath to approach his Lord – to ask

questions about these changes. In the end he did not have to. His Lord came rolling up to him. There was spray and spume about him. The boy was grinding the edge of his sword, whetting it to a fine edge.

'Things are different now, I think. My friend with the raven plans to help us make camp over winter to be closer to the soft fat lands of the south. You and I, boy, will have gold and slaves enough to last us long!'

He explained.

The ragtag chief was a friend from long ago. He had been landless and lacked status though he was mightily ambitious. They had joined forces – for the spoil. They took a village for their own – killing all within. He was thus able to petition the king to have it handed to him. The king by law was unable to prevent this. He knew nothing of the raid. And so the once landless warrior now had lands and holdings of his own. Now he was looking to expand them. This was the reason then for us heading so far south and ignoring possibilities of plunder along the way.

The boy regarded once again the newcomer. He was deep in conversation with his raven stroking and gentling the feathers that were being ruffled by the sea wind.

A feeling came over him of sadness and despair as

clouds obscured his vision. Shapes and shadows filled his head. There was a clamour of voices behind him and he whirled round to confront the sound only to discover that he was alone. He gripped his sword trying to stave off the fears that began to overwhelm him. The sounds in his head grew louder. The visions more compelling. He rose, staggered and cried out, falling in a crumpled heap onto the timbers. Friends rushed forward, concerned for him. They raised him up, forced water through white lips and were startled to see him staring straight through them at some vision of which only he was aware.

His breath came in great ragged gasps as he watched the procession of events unfold before him. And ever and above them the girl's face beseeching and imploring and he helpless and powerless.

At last the boy's mind quieted. His breathing became easier and his eyes closed. He slept. He was laid gently away from careless feet, covered and left to come to in his own time.

The ship sailed on southwards, the sun high in the sky now and the wind pushing them on. The great raven on the sail bellied out over the dragonhead on the prow. The stranger and his bird were disdainful of the commotion behind them and continued to watch the sea as it surged round the boat rattling over the sides and gently ebbing away below.

The boat rode the waters like a great horse, easy and restful on the back of the swell using its power to carry it forward before the wind.

The boy slept on.

CHAPTER TWENTY-TWO

I awoke to darkness and quiet. Though it was not completely quiet. That was what had wakened me. The baby crying loudly but quickly hushed. My husband stirred beside me, came back to wakefulness but then slipped back into sleep and was still. I lay listening in the grey light that comes before dawn hearing nothing but my own thoughts which tumbled ceaselessly through my head not coming to rest anywhere. I was so very tired, too tired almost to continue the battle that raged surreptitiously around me.

The baby's mother was openly hostile now sure of her position. There were many who sided with her and had no time for me, still a stranger from the woods.

And yet childless.

Though I feared that this may no longer be so.

My body was changing, adapting itself to care for the new life that was in me for certain.

I did not want this child. Did not want the burden placed upon me by bringing it to life. Let that other baby take on its father's mantle. I who did not belong, did not want to belong, would not be responsible for creating such a life.

As I lay thinking and wondering what I should do, I felt my husband's hands reach for me but I moved away and slipped from the bed. He murmured sleepily but let me go. Since that night he'd had more care for me. Almost it was as if he regretted the passion aroused and sated in me.

I moved to the cooking fires and helped bring them to strength and heat ready for the demanding bellies that would soon roar to be filled.

But I was listless and distracted and my heart was not in my work. I moved away, stood by the door and watched the lightening of the sky. The breeze came in from the sea and I lifted my head scenting the air questing like some beast searching for quarry but I knew not for what I was searching, only that I searched. I ached with the loneliness of the void that was in me.

The first waves of nausea washed over me and

took me unawares. I retched, drawing away from the open doorway that no-one should see and guess. I would not keep this life within my body. I knew that now. There was urgency. I needed herbs. I needed wise words to help me expel the life from my body.

The old woman! She would know. But would she keep my secret? To whom did she truly owe allegiance? Though she had clucked over me as an old hen might her runty chick, still she was not of my blood or of my hearth. I would need to choose careful words. But words I must speak and speak soon.

The retching subsided and I straightened, leaning on the doorframe as I waited for the shivering to cease and my strength to return before I re-entered the hall. Taking huge calming breaths I felt the warmth being drawn into my limbs and I turned.

With a start I found myself looking directly into the eyes of the old woman. She had seen me and watched me and would know. I froze momentarily but then she moved towards me with open arms and I fell forward, grateful for the encircling safety of her love. A mother's love. How I had missed my mother. I sobbed and was soothed by her murmurings of comfort and care and her hands stroking me gently to quiet.

She knew without being told what was in my heart

and she knew also the herbs that would bring an end to the changes in my body. Though sad for me and for my husband and for the small thing growing inside of me, she would give me herbs. Patting my hands finally she turned and softly she left me.

In a daze I looked about me. I went into the hall. I could not eat and found even the smells from the fires unbearable.

CHAPTER TWENTY-THREE

It was later that same day when the old woman found me at my loom and led me away from my work. I followed unresisting as she searched out a corner of the hall that was all in shadow.

She sat and looked at me very carefully before asking if I was sure of what my heart was telling me. She wanted to know that my secrets would be safe, would always be so. She knew, she said, what it was to carry unwanted life. Her face twisted painfully at some old memory. Whether of her own or another's pain, I knew not.

And then she spoke, her voice scarce above a whisper.

'Once, very many years ago I was young and loved. My life was set and the pattern of it was dear to me.

My husband though chosen for me was kind and loved me in his way.

'A spring day it was when I ventured alone to the strand in search of crabs or some such even though to do this was discouraged. There were marauders along the coast but being young I paid no heed to the warnings.

'I did not hear over the roar of the surf footsteps on the shingle. They were moving quietly and I was unaware of danger until my arms were cruelly pinned to my body and I was hauled up. I felt the screams rise in my throat only to be cut off by a powerful grip on my mouth. I was spun around so I could see my captors and stare them in the face. I shall never forget the gleam in their eyes. The animal stink of their breath as it poured over me.'

The old woman paused her eyes turned inward reliving her agony, unable to go on. Silence stretched between us. I took her hands in my own and felt the dry brittleness of old age and sadness in the thin fingers. I said nothing and at last with a great effort she came back to me smiling sadly.

'There were three of them.

'They left me bleeding and torn where I lay at the edge of the tide. My clothes became sodden and the blood was washed from me before I was able to move. Darkness was all around as I gathered myself together.

'My mind was dazed and my eyes unseeing so that I stumbled, adding to my injuries. Though furious my husband was unable to do anything other than rant at me for being so careless and unheeding. It was as if he blamed me. That it was my fault.

'When my belly began to swell he turned from me.'

She was silent again. Thoughtful.

'The child died. Tearing its way from my body it strangled and never breathed and I was glad.'

Starkly she ended.

'There were no more children.'

I waited.

'It was a very long time ago.'

Her sadness passed and her mind returned to the present and the matter in hand. She brought boiling water and stewed the herbs for me. The scent was not unpleasant. There were no more second thoughts. I must do this. At her urging I drank deeply.

'The pains will start tonight. Keep your own counsel and tell no-one what has passed here.'

She left me then and though anxious I knew I should be careful and not attract attention to myself.

I spent the rest of the day at my loom unnoticed by any and approached by none. My loneliness and isolation seemed complete. I felt tears sting my eyes but I would not allow them to fall.

At day's end my husband went straight to the baby and his mother. I felt nothing. Somehow the numbness that had possessed me and sustained me in the forest filled me once more.

But who would take it away this time?

I was alone.

CHAPTER TWENTY-FOUR

Avoiding headlands, rocks and shifting sands the small fleet of boats continued on their southward course. Blessed by a following wind, progress was swift.

The boy sat by the steersman with a line in his hand pulling up fat fish which were immediately gutted and put to dry in the sun by men who were not needed for rowing. Screaming gulls chased through the wind to snap at glittering scraps.

The boats flew on.

One morning there was movement and excitement. Fingers were pointed to a beach above which could be seen ancient buildings long since abandoned. Men were everywhere stowing oars and securing masts with shouts and curses ringing in their ears. Others leapt over the side hauling ropes and running up onto the beach where they commenced to dragging the ship over the shingle. Boats came to a shuddering stop and lay there as men stretched and stamped their feet on the stones regaining their balance for the land.

The boy looked about him. The sun was above the horizon and the sky was clear. Fires were smoking and flaring up as cooking pots were filled and hung over the flames. He noticed his Lord walking away and apart with the brute and his raven. Heads together, they were lost in thought. Should he join them – would they resent the intrusion? But no – he would wait.

There was an uneasy quiet in the camp and the men were subdued. The boy filled his belly, stretched and looked about him. It seemed to him that this shore was familiar. Memories surfaced and he felt them unfold in his mind. Some were fleeting and could not be caught and of course those were the ones the boy wanted to catch.

He lay back against a rock and closed his eyes fully, allowing the memories to clear and fill his head. A young girl. An old woman. Fear and pain.

His eyes flew open and he leapt up. This was the shore that he had walked along with the old woman when he was returning to life. This was the rock on which he had sat contemplating the future.

Breathing deeply and shaking, he stood quietly. He must know what happened to the old woman. He must know what happened to his village.

His Lord must let him go. He would wait for him to return and ask permission.

CHAPTER TWENTY-FIVE

The day wore on in a drowsy fashion. There was quiet and rest for those who had so recently been busy and games of chance for those who needed to pass the time. The boy, wrapped in his cloak, dozed and dreamed.

His dreams were full of shadows and shapes swirling through cloud. Ravens were there and a pair of sad green eyes saw him through the clouds. He awoke with a start to noise and shouting as his Lord returned – alone though leading a string of horses and ponies. Men moved to set up horse lines under the trees at the forest's edge and the beasts were left to crop what grass they could reach.

The boy stood up and waited for the milling men to settle and the noise to recede. His Lord strode up to him.

'You know this place.'

It wasn't a question.

The boy nodded as his Lord gazed upon him through hooded eyelids.

'There is a village near. We will go there, you and I.'

He turned and shouted for horses and guards.

The boy took the reins of a small chestnut mare that danced on her toes, eager to be off. He quieted her and waited for the Lord who seemed to be struggling rather and out of breath as he finally heaved himself up onto the back of his heavy, grey horse. He sat for a moment and then yanking the reins wheeled round and made for the trees. The boy followed more quietly after the warriors who jostled each other as they entered the forest, uneasy on the swaying backs of horses, preferring the heaving of a wooden ship under their feet.

The boy searched between the trunks of trees thick and hoary with age as his mare picked her way precisely through the undergrowth. There was no path here, he was unsure of his bearings and there was no chance to explore further. He was in no position to petition his Lord for time to search. The Lord's wishes were paramount after all.

Eventually they heard noise towards which they turned.

And there in the clearing was the boy's village.

He stopped his mare who snorted at being left behind. He shook and sweat poured down his body. His eyes closed and he swayed in the saddle before a shout roused him and returned him to his senses.

'Boy – come here now!'

Reluctantly the boy urged on his mare. He caught up with his Lord who gazed at him without speaking for a moment. The boy held his gaze even as his mind swirled in confusion.

'This was your village, was it not?'

He nodded.

'Much changed, I think, since you were last through this gate.'

And he laughed – though not unkindly.

CHAPTER TWENTY-SIX

Walking through the gate with the others the boy noticed many changes since last he was there. The hall still stood though now it was run down and unkempt. The new masters obviously had little time for maintaining appearances. The huts also were showing signs of decay as if there were still no families to use them and they remained empty and sad.

The boy was overcome with memories which threatened to overwhelm him but he stayed straight in the saddle and would not let any see how he was affected.

Approaching the hall the group came to a halt and waited. They did not have to wait long. Pushing his way through the hall and out into the gathering gloom, the new owner of the village and the lands about emerged and regarded the group through half-closed eyes.

The boy swallowed but kept his feelings hidden. Now was not the time to make any kind of fuss.

His Lord slipped from his horse a little unsteadily but regained his balance as he moved forwards into the embrace of his friend.

'Welcome all – welcome to my Hall, my friends! Enter and drink – eat your fill and rest for the night! But perhaps not so much rest, eh?' And he laughed and his warriors laughed also. The boy did not.

He stepped over the threshold into the gloom keeping himself hidden in the shadows whilst he took in his surroundings. So much was changed and his heart sank. There seemed to be ghosts in the shadows with him – sad, quiet ghosts and the boy was still as if he listened to their silent voices.

Eventually he followed his fellows into the firelight, breathing deeply and evenly and the ghosts were left in the shadows unable to follow. He felt the lightest of touches on his shoulder and he turned quickly but no-one was there – of course.

CHAPTER TWENTY-SEVEN

The boy sat on a bench with some of those who had travelled with him and they talked quietly, wondering why they were there. They ate well and filled their bellies. And waited.

His Lord and the Outlaw were roaring and shouting and clapping each other on the back. The raven flapped through the smoke and the noise was great. The boy felt a tightness behind his eyes and making his excuses he made his way to the door, pushing aside the leather curtain and breathing in the fresh air gratefully.

The sky was dark, with shining points of light dancing slowly through the heavens giving a gentle glow to the land on which the boy stood. All was still and the boy let his thoughts wander through the trees and the starlight and his head cleared.

He returned to the hall which was now settling for the night and he found a corner where he could lay his fur and sleep although this eluded him for some time.

CHAPTER TWENTY-EIGHT

And then the sky was lightening and there was bustle and fuss as warriors and outlaws alike gathered furs and weapons stopping only to slake their thirst and relieve themselves against the walls of the building before grabbing their horses and mounting, in readiness to ride wherever their Lords should say.

The boy looked at his Lord who sat his horse uneasily and whose breathing was becoming laboured as he waited for the Outlaw and his small band of men to join them. Others too had noticed their Lord's demeanour and were looking about them in some consternation until at last the Outlaw rode up with a clatter of sword on shield and drew their eyes away.

His Lord straightened and turning to the boy who was as ever, close by, spoke.

'Well lad, it would seem that there is a village over the hill there that might just be worth visiting – what d'you say, eh? Shall we go and show them the ways of the Northmen?' And he laughed and was once more the Lord that the boy knew.

He smiled with relief but still there was a worry in his head as he went to find his horse.

Riding through the trees in single file the warriors were quiet and thinking thoughts of their own but having faith and trust in their leader were unafraid.

Sunlight slanted down on moss and grass which looked inviting to horses but they were too well-disciplined to notice and walked on, on their neat little hooves, making hardly a mark in the soft carpet under the trees.

There was a halt by a clear brook that tumbled over round, smooth pebbles. The horses stood in the cool water and drank thirstily swishing their tails against the swarms of midges that were plaguing them. Men dismounted and joined them in the water before clambering onto the banks and searching amongst their packs for hard bread or perhaps a heel of cheese that had been overlooked at another time. Unlucky ones cursed and flopped down beside their horses which were now able to enjoy the sweet grass.

There was quiet for a time as the day passed.

And then there was movement among the trees and the Northmen gathered together. The Outlaw was leading his band with the raven on his shoulder and the Lord seemed content that it was so. Looking at him the boy thought he seemed distracted and quiet. There were no roars or loud words but none of the others thought anything amiss.

One of the scouts suddenly burst onto the path, startling the boy out of his reverie. There were warriors up ahead. Swords were gripped and reins were tightened.

After talking together the Viking and the Outlaw drew their men into lines and bid us all be still – we were not ready for battle yet but would fight if we must.

It was warm under the trees and only the buzz of insects broke the silence. The very air was holding its breath then at once there was a shift and all relaxed. There was a whispered conversation then we were turned away to retreat further into the forest.

After some time we dismounted. The Lord came to his men and spoke.

'There is plunder nearby, my fine warriors, and it is in my mind for us to have a share. We will return to the boats and make ready.' And with that he mounted his horse and wheeled round back the way they came. The boy followed – what else could he do?

The group of warriors was not so silent on the way back as they talked of other battles and skirmishes in which they had fought – oh so very bravely! There was no talk of the fear that comes upon every man when raising his sword and calling upon Odin and Thor. No talk of the pain of seeing those who were cut down, or of the screams of the horses as they slipped and slid on the flesh of men and animals.

No – the boy knew all about battle and fear. His gut tightened at the memories with which he was assailed and he waited for what was to come.

An echo of a face drifted through his mind and he shut his eyes trying to stop it from leaving but he was unable. He sighed.

Their progress back to the shoreline was hurried and once there they all returned to where they had stowed their gear and food.

'Tonight we eat and sleep – tomorrow we fight. Isn't that so, my friend?' The raven swooped down from the Outlaw's shoulder and looked at the Lord with an unblinking eye. The bird made the boy uneasy and he looked away making as if to find food to fill his belly. The Outlaw also made him uneasy. He could not understand why his Lord was friend to him. But for now all was well and they were filled with anticipation, of plundering and killing and filling their boats to sail home leaving the Outlaw with plunder enough and new land to plough. And slaves. Of course there would always be slaves. The Outlaw professed to want slaves more than gold or furs. His band could grow – become powerful and important and he would no longer be the Outlaw.

The Outlaw band returned to their Hall for the night, leaving the Vikings camped by the shore.

There were no fires that night and no hot food but the night was warm. There were no stories – no songs – and there would be fighting enough tomorrow. The camp slept.

The boy lay on his back and gazed up at the stars trying to make sense of the fleeting visions and thoughts in his head but he could not. He closed his eyes then and slept.

CHAPTER TWENTY-NINE

The girl was weaving but the work was difficult today and she was unable to settle. She looked around but no-one was looking at her. No-one looked at her any more very much. Only the old woman was still her friend though even she had to be careful. As long as the girl was useful she was safe but she knew that that would change if she was no longer able to prove her worth.

The chief – no longer chief's son now – had not sought her bed for many nights since she lost the child she was carrying. He blamed her for that and she had to admit to herself that he was right to do so but she could not have kept the child, not here in this hall.

Her fingers stilled and fell in her lap as she felt a great sadness overwhelm her as she thought that this would be her life from now on. Living in the shadows

– being quiet – wanting not to be noticed. Not even being able to visit the small child she had saved though she was happy he was well and thriving. It was a small success and she was able to smile at that.

Taking a deep breath she took up her work again. It went more easily this time. As the day wore on the girl was aware of a change in the atmosphere. There was tension and she could hear raised voices. She concentrated on the words that she could hear, without stopping her work.

'I tell you it's the same band that was here last time – and they laid waste to villages all around! We cannot let them stay close to us here!'

'We will have to fight – your father would fight!'

She carefully turned her head at this insult to the chief – he would not let this go unchallenged. The hall was quiet as all looked to the chief whose skin had flushed at this insult.

'We will fight, make no mistake, if this sorry band of rogues and outlaws should come close, but I am not willing to sacrifice men's lives for nothing. We watch and we wait!'

He turned abruptly and left the hall shouting for his horse.

Peace returned to the hall, although it was an uneasy peace as men followed their chief, pushing and grumbling, into the sunlight. Knots of women gathered by the hearth-fire talking and worrying. The girl was not invited to join them.

She looked up as the old woman sidled up to her, speaking softly.

'It would seem that the Northern bastards are at our gates once more, Odin damn them!'

Her tone of voice belied the vehemence of the words she spat out and the girl was startled.

'Surely we are safe here – there are many warriors? My own village was not so well-protected – but her...'

Her words drifted into the shadows and were silenced.

'No-one and nowhere is safe. I will tell you what news I am able.'

Her words were cut short as the chief's woman gave way to hysterics and her cries filled the air. She collapsed, sobbing into the arms of her serving-women who were uncertain what to do about this unseemly show. They shushed her and stroked her and brought her ale.

And the day passed.

CHAPTER THIRTY

The chief was not seen again until late in the evening when the Hall was filled with the quiet murmurings of people wanting to settle for the night but who were too anxious. He stalked in with a thunderous expression on his face and his men at his shoulder shouting instructions about what he should be doing.

'Enough!' he roared. 'I will sleep tonight and we will fight tomorrow! That should please all here!' And he gazed round his Hall.

His glance fell on the girl and she shrank into the shadows with her eyes downcast hoping that he would not notice her. Her body flooded with relief when she saw the old woman go to him with a drinking horn.

'My Lord!' she cried. 'You must be thirsty...' There was a moment then when it seemed as though he might push her away and make for the girl but thinking better of it he took the horn and drained it, turning away to the fire demanding food. The women scuttled around giving him a full bowl and bread, filling his horn with more ale.

The old woman made her way slowly taking a circuitous route back to the girl, not wanting to arouse curiosity or draw eyes in her direction. As she drew level with the corner in which she had secreted herself she smiled.

'All is well now – he will have other things to think of and will forget about you once again. Sleep now while you are able. Tomorrow may bring sorrow and death.' She sighed heavily. 'There is never an end to sorrow and death. It is wyrd – we may not know when death will come for us.' She sat and looked at the girl who had wrapped herself in a fur ready to sleep and gently stroked her cheek.

'Death holds no horror for me but you, my mysterious elf from the forest, should not have to be thinking of such things yet. We will await the morrow and see then what the chief decides. He will have to attack the Northmen or risk losing his place as chief amongst us and that he will not do.'

There was noise around the fire as the chief's

woman tried to lure him to her sleeping place but he brushed her off and looked round as if there was something gnawing at him. The girl held her breath and remained motionless waiting for him to be distracted. Then she turned to the old woman having made a decision.

'I cannot stay here this night – I will not be safe and I am unable to bear the thought of him putting his hands on me once more. I know where I may hide but I shall not tell you. You will be able to truthfully say that you have no knowledge of me.' And she smiled. 'Thank you, old woman, for all that you have been to me and I wish you well in the coming days.'

The two clasped each other in the darkness knowing that it would be the last time and cried quietly.

The girl slipped away and the old woman felt her heart breaking.

CHAPTER THIRTY-ONE

It was a moonless night but the girl made her way to the hut at the edge of the forest without stumbling. She had visited often to see the child as he grew. He seemed content and his parents were grateful for her help. They had named the baby Durwyn.

She told them to prepare for a journey and that they would hide in the forest before the fighting that was surely only hours away.

'But where can we hide safely and what of Durwyn?'

'Give him to me. You bring food to tide us over until we are safe.'

'But our chief – our friends and our cattle?'

'There is no time and it may be that the chief and his warriors will die in the fighting. Come – we have little time to spare.'

She hurried round the small hut chivvying the reluctant family until at last they were ready. It had not taken long. The night was still dark but she was sure that there was a lightening of the sky in the east.

The village was just beginning to stir as they hastened through the gate towards the trees. Luckily the guard was in the Hall with the other men so they did not have to invent a reason for leaving. The girl had been worried about this and was relieved. She clutched Durwyn tightly to her and he mewled in protest, eyes screwed tightly shut. He was a sturdy child and once again the girl was glad and happy in the knowledge that he had saved him from what would have been certain death had he been left with his mother. She cuddled him closer and he was quiet at last.

The little group reached the safety of the trees and paused for a while looking back at their village. The girl felt nothing but relief to escape although the old woman tugged at her heart and she worried for her, though she had her blessing which meant much.

The sky was lightening and the village was stirring. It was time to go.

CHAPTER THIRTY-TWO

The sun had only just risen over the horizon when the boy awoke with a hollow feeling in the pit of his stomach. He was unsure of what the day would bring and was less than eager to shrug off the sleep which had finally claimed him.

His Lord was everywhere urging his men to hurry.

'Up! Up, you fighters – you warriors! We will reach that village before those weaklings have pissed on the midden!' And he laughed.

There was little grumbling as the Northmen saddled their horses and checked their weapons. Their minds were focused and they made no noise as they went about the task in hand. Bread was handed out, and ale. It might be some time before they would be able to fill their bellies so they ate well.

The boy too ate though found the bread sticking in his throat. He washed it down with drafts of ale and coughed. His Lord came up and clapped him on the back causing him to lurch against his horse who stepped back quickly snorting.

'Steady there, my warrior! It were best you don't injure yourself before the battle! There will be time enough for wounds later!'

And with a great roar of laughter he strode off, his eyes everywhere seeing everything and all was well with him. He was content.

The boy finished his bread and thought to tuck some amongst his clothes. It might be needed later. He would find water if he could. After the battle.

He sighed.

The day grew lighter and the warriors lined up in single file to travel swiftly through the forest. The two men left to guard the boats waved farewell with shouts of good luck, calling on Odin and Thor to fight alongside them, bringing them victory and glory so that songs would be sung about them at hearths in years to come.

The boy walked his horse close by his Lord and was alarmed to hear him breathing loudly and rubbing his chest as if there was some discomfort there.

'My Lord – are you ill? Should we go back? We don't have to fight this day.'

'Yes we do, I think. I must not let my friend see that I am ill. He is perhaps not such a good friend.' He smiled sadly. 'We will meet soon and then we shall see, shall we not?' He sat straighter in his saddle and lifted his head seeming to sniff the breeze.

'Ah – I think I hear them. Come on, boy – to battle…'

Swinging his horse round the Lord sat and waited for the Outlaw and his band and then there they were. There was a noise of greeting and laughing though quiet, there under the trees.

The raven sat comfortably on the Outlaw's shoulder, unconcerned and unconcerning.

'So, my Northman – we fight! For land and slaves! This is what I want – and you – you have whatever precious stuff is there and what you can pack back into your boats and take home to the north.'

There was no great noise or beating of shields, however, the time for noise and clamour would be soon enough when the village was in sight. Until then all was quiet as they trotted slowly through the forest.

The boy looked about him noticing how old the

trees must be by the way that branches were gnarled and twisted, roots heaving up through the earth. The sun had to struggle to reach the ground but where it did there was soft moss and grass and close by a small stream which caught the dancing sunlight as it filtered through the leaves.

And his thoughts drifted once more but now he thought of the old woman who had healed him so very long ago. She would no longer be there in her hut near the shore and he hoped that her end had been peaceful. He smiled in recollection of her kindness.

And so the morning passed.

CHAPTER THIRTY-THREE

The girl and the little family she was intent on saving had travelled away from their village following well-worn paths and the going was easy. They stopped. Durwyn was put down onto the grass where he wriggled around glad to be free of constraining arms. He grinned and the girl grinned back feeling her heart lighten momentarily. He was a lovely child and she hoped he would be safe – that they would all be safe.

After some searching in their packs food was found and shared. A clear stream was near and they drank.

'We must leave the path now and you must follow me closely as some of the way will be hard but my cave is not far.'

'Cave?' asked the woman. 'What caves are there

here? I know of none.'

The girl shuddered at her memories and went on.

'When I ran from the Vikings and my home, and all that I loved, I found an earth cave under a great oak tree which sheltered me for many months. It was dry and large. There was water close by. We will be hidden.'

'I don't know,' said the man. 'This seems strange to us.' And he glanced at his wife looking to her for confirmation that what they were about to do was right.

She nodded.

'Come,' she said, gathering Durwyn, 'we must hurry. We can't linger. We are sure to be missed in the village.' She turned to look back the way they had come then taking a deep breath she determinedly set her face towards the forest and moved forward. Her husband followed looking around to ensure that nothing of their passing was left.

The girl led them deeper into the forest and they tried hard not to be disquieted by the gloom and stillness around. It seemed as though the forest and all in it were holding their breath, watching their progress. The girl was comforted by the quiet – it had once been her friend and had sheltered her for all the time she had been hidden there.

Evening was drawing on when suddenly the girl raised her arm bringing them to a halt.

'See — there by the great tree — there is the cave!' She pointed to the darkness that could be seen through the undergrowth which grew high at this time of year.

Husband and wife followed her gaze and saw the dense blackness which caused the woman to cry out.

'That? But that's not even large enough for Durwyn never mind the three of us!'

She rounded on the girl.

'To where have you brought us? We'll perish here if not from sword stroke then from starvation! What can we do — what can we do?' And she sank down to the forest floor weeping. Durwyn cried also knowing instinctively that his mother was alarmed. Her husband joined her there and looked at the girl with worry in his eyes.

'Please — all will be well,' she said beseechingly. 'We have food — there is water. We will not long be here. Battles will be fought and killing will be done with! We have but to wait...' Her voice tailed off and her hands hung by her side as she gazed imploringly at the couple on the ground.

There was silence then a deep sigh.

'We have no choice.' The woman's voice was quiet but resigned as she clung to her husband's arm. He raised her up whilst she shushed Durwyn who finally stilled his crying.

Pushing aside the overgrowth they entered the cave, standing near the entrance whilst their eyes adjusted to the gloom.

'See,' said the girl, 'there is room enough here for a short while.'

She looked round seeing and remembering her time here although much of her memory was hazy. It had not been a good time.

The cave went right under the tree which must surely come down one day in the not too distant future when the wind blew just a little too hard and the rain fell just a little too unceasingly but for now they were safe and all that could be heard were the snuffles of a hungry Durwyn and the beating of hearts which were heavy with fear and worry for what tomorrow and the days after might bring.

CHAPTER THIRTY-FOUR

There was confusion and bustle in the village, and fear. Men were shouting at each other, unsure of what must be done when they had a chief who was unwilling to stand up to the heathen from the north. Some were about to come to blows when the chief swept in and shoved them asunder.

'Enough! Now is not the time! I have had word that the Viking band has been joined by the outlaws that settled the girl's village that was destroyed!' He looked around with a puzzled expression. 'Where is she? I saw her last evening but now...' He let her slip from his mind. He would think about her later. There was fighting and slaughter to be done.

Women were quick to help the men collect their weapons and shields. All had battle axes tucked securely into their belts and many had swords which were precious to them. Bread was brought round and horns of ale and the men ate. The chief did not. His insides were roiling and not able to be still so he drank instead and wished his father still with him.

His gaze landed on his son sitting over by the fire. He was enjoying the fuss and grinning, his little fists in the air. The chief smiled at him and felt a wave of something wash over him — sadness, wyrd — he knew not but he knew that this day would be his last and felt himself unmanned.

Breathing deeply he rose from his seat by the fire and gathering his warriors with his eyes made for the doorway leaving silence behind him. Even the child was quiet as if he knew...

The horses were brought and the chief mounted, his heart heavy. He turned for a final glimpse of his son playing in the firelight and suddenly remembered the other son — where was he? He shook his head. It was becoming more difficult to think and he must have a clear head if he was to lead his men safely through the forest.

He pulled up his horse shortly after leaving the village, peering into the trees wondering which way he should be heading. His men were restless. The horses were shifting uneasily and he knew that he must decide.

Turning his horse to the left then and kicking him on they were soon amongst the trees. The moss underfoot was soft and muffled the sound of their passing. Ears were alert for any sound but even the creatures of the forest were silent this day and there was little to hear but breathing and stillness.

They passed a gnarled and aged oak not far from their path. It looked familiar but the chief was not able to say why this was so. It slipped from his mind so he was never after able to answer two of the questions he had asked himself earlier.

He and his men passed on and did not see the pair of bright eyes hidden in the tangle of roots, following them as they went.

The girl held her breath. So close they were – so close and yet they had moved on and her little band was safe for a little longer.

CHAPTER THIRTY-FIVE

The band of warriors and outlaws had come together and made a fearsome group as they travelled through the forest uncaring of the noise and hiatus they might create.

In a clearing a halt was called as the leaders talked together and the boy could hear the Outlaw's roaring laugh and his Lord's more caring response to the man's suggestions. The great raven flapped and squawked and seemed to look right at him with his bright terrifying eyes. The boy shuddered. This was not his battle. He had no wish to fight villagers who were only protecting their herds and their families. They were not warriors. They could not fight and they would die. Did he want to be a part of that? He did not think so.

He needed to think.

Hanging back from the main body of men he let his horse wallow and slake his thirst in the stream that ran by the path while he thought. He knew his Lord might let him go after his years of service but he was not so sure about the Outlaw. The Outlaw was cunning and he would not trust anyone who had no stomach for a fight thinking that they were traitors and should be killed without any more ado.

He returned to his Lord.

'I recognise this part of the forest I think, my Lord. I shall go and see if I am right if that should please you. I may find a clearer way for us.'

He waited. The Outlaw spoke.

'So young warrior, you know this place?'

'I may do.' He paused. 'I knew someone once who lived close by I think.'

The boy spoke carefully and kept his body relaxed not wishing to give the Outlaw cause to take more notice of him wondering what might be in his head.

Whilst thinking, the Outlaw absentmindedly stroked his raven who sat on his shoulder with closed eyes.

'I have not seen my pet for many weeks,' observed the Viking wistfully. 'I trust that he is well and will be there when I return home to the north.' And he moved to stroke the bird which opened his eyes wide, snapping viciously at this hand. The Viking jumped back in alarm and his men muttered.

'This is an evil bird indeed! Not like mine own at all!' He sucked crossly at the wound which was seeping bright blood between his fingers.

'He mistrusts all. Not unlike myself in fact,' the Outlaw said quietly, looking at his friend through suspicious eyes.

Hands went to weapons and reins were tightened in readiness for defence of their leaders but the Outlaw laughed and the tension eased.

'Go then, boy – and find us an easy way through this forest. And be quick about it.'

The boy looked to his Lord who nodded and smiled gently at him.

'Yes – it may yet save us time and afford us an advantage when we finally meet the village warriors. They will be looking for us along the path. They will not expect us to come through the forest a different way.'

The boy pulled his reluctant horse off into the forest and was soon lost to view.

CHAPTER THIRTY-SIX

As he wandered through the undergrowth the boy was thinking and wondering what he would do if he came across the villagers. They were only trying to defend themselves after all, as had his village all that time ago. He remembered well the devastation, and the sense of loss that afflicted him for so long after. His sympathies were not with the raiders. He was tired of bloodshed and death. He thought perhaps that he might not find them after all.

He turned off the path and his horse slowed as the undergrowth became more tangled and dense. There was quiet and stillness here in the depths of the forest. Sunlight was fitful and shifting. The horse slowed and bent his head taking this chance to gather mouthfuls of grass from between his feet. His rider was still and thoughtful.

There was a movement then over to his left and the boy's eyes were immediately drawn to what he thought might be deer or possibly boar. His senses quickened and he pulled on his reins in readiness for flight. He had no wish to upset any boar that might call these woods home. But his horse was quiet and not at all nervous so it could not possibly be boar. The boy looked hard at the movement and waited.

CHAPTER THIRTY-SEVEN

'Stay here – I will see what I can, now the forest is quiet.'

The girl pushed aside the covering of briers that she had used to camouflage their refuge and carefully climbed out emerging into silence. There was no sound of warriors passing and no sign that any were nearby.

Breathing a great sigh of relief she clambered out and stretched. It had been hard staying still under the great oak and very uncomfortable. It was fortunate that Durwyn was such a quiet baby who seemed very content as long as his tummy was full. She smiled when she thought of him. He was a very sweet little boy. What was to become of him? What was to become of her? Or any of them? She sighed again and felt weighed down with worry but she raised her head at last and looked through the trees searching for she knew not what.

CHAPTER THIRTY-EIGHT

The boy stopped his horse and listened. The day was drawing on and he knew that he really should not wander through the forest when night fell but he was unsure whether to return to the Viking band. And if he did not – what then? He felt a tug on the reins as his mount grazed on the rich grass beneath his hooves. He followed the animal aimlessly until it stopped suddenly and threw up its head, ears pricked and eyes staring into the gloom.

The boy's hand moved immediately to his sword as he crouched, turning his head to follow the direction of his horse's gaze. He and the animal were quite still. There was the sound of a soft footfall.

Then the world stopped turning.

CHAPTER THIRTY-NINE

Resisting the urge to scream the girl stiffened as she felt her blood turn to ice in her veins. Her senses failed her and she crumpled to the ground.

The boy ran forward and fell to his knees, shaking so that he thought he would never stop. He clasped the girl's hands, tears falling on her upturned palms. She opened her eyes which were blank and unfocussed. Her breath came in ragged gasps, as did his. Neither could believe who had appeared before them and neither seemed able to move and break the spell.

There was a mewling cry swiftly shushed and the girl shook her head at last.

'I must go – the child...' She scrambled up and turned to go.

The boy held her arm.

'Wait...'

CHAPTER FORTY

The girl fell into the hole in a tumble unable to arrange the swirling thoughts that likewise tumbled through her head.

'He's alive. He's alive. He's…' And then she stopped as three terrified pairs of eyes looked at her in horrified amazement.

There was silence.

And then a crashing as the boy dragged his horse after the girl, desperate not to lose her again now that he had found her. His breath was hoarse and painful as he tried to make sense of what was happening. He stopped at the entrance to the hide, searching through the gloom. He could only see what seemed to be a bundle of rags and then he saw the wriggling form of Durwyn who was the first to recover and started crying.

The man pushed his way out and confronted the boy even though his chest was heaving and it was paining him.

'What is this? Who are you?'

The boy stepped back and began to explain or try to, when the girl raised herself up to speak. The woman hushed Durwyn and waited.

'I knew him once. I thought he was dead, long ago and now he is here.' She shook her head wonderingly, still not believing that this could happen – had happened.

The boy reached out his hand and the girl took his fingers in hers feeling the strength and warmth there and she was quiet.

'He was from my village. The Northmen came…' Her voice tailed off. Nothing more needed to be said. She looked at the boy who had a question in his eyes.

'No – the child is not mine.' She smiled.

CHAPTER FORTY-ONE

After silence all was confusion and bustle.

'There are bands of warriors in the forest — we can't stay.' The boy looked at the little group of fugitives in front of him, tired and frightened. It was hopeless, he supposed. But as he looked, he remembered.

'I know of a place. It's not far. Once it saved and protected me though I doubt my saviour still lives. We must go.'

The girl wasted no time. She trusted the boy. They were together at last and her heart was finally at peace. It was a strange feeling after all this time. As she collected her few things she gave a last thought to the village and the people who had sheltered her. The young Lord who had saved her from the forest only to frighten and overwhelm her when she could not or would not love him. The spiteful girl whose abandoned baby now shared her life.

The old woman who had helped her and cared for her so lovingly. She was the only one for whom she had any feelings. She had been so very kind. She wondered what might happen to them all. Was one of those bands of warriors made up of those villagers? She rather thought it might.

CHAPTER FORTY-TWO

The villagers had followed paths through the forest for some time and many of them were becoming restless. Their chief and Lord was not behaving as such and not land they were afraid and insecure. They needed direction. They needed to know what to do if they came across the Northmen. Their chief had let them down. There were mutterings and irritations. Their chief knew this and his mind gave way, finally.

He dismounted and stood trembling. The group stopped and observed him. There was little sympathy. He was no longer their chief. He wept and sank to the ground. And as he wept he thought of the strange girl from the forest and the baby son he had left behind and its twin who must surely be dead. And his father who had left him too soon. It was too much and he was unsurprised as he felt the blow to his head and he welcomed the darkness.

CHAPTER FORTY-THREE

The villagers turned from their chief and left him there, crumpled and destroyed. Riding along the green pathways they were thoughtful. They realised that they had done a desperate thing to leave their chief so. Would their village still be waiting after the coming fight? No-one knew.

They drew swords or clutched spears and held on tightly to their shields. Horses were restive. They could hear other horses beyond in the clearing and now the one who had taken it upon himself to lead, dashed forward through the trees with a great scream.

CHAPTER FORTY-FOUR

The Northmen gathered in a clearing. The Outlaw looked at his friend and stroked the raven who sat quietly on his shoulder.

'And where is your young friend? He has been gone long enough I think. Do you trust him? I am not sure that I do.'

'I trust the boy.'

And then there was noise.

CHAPTER FORTY-FIVE

The warrior band whirled, preparing to repel these bothersome villagers but they were surprised by the ferocity of their attack and almost before they were aware the first blows had been struck.

CHAPTER FORTY-SIX

The boy hurried the girl and the couple along. He had no need to urge them to quiet. They were silent. Fear driving them forwards.

At hearing a commotion in the distance the boy stopped them and took them into a stand of trees.

'Wait – I will go and watch what is happening. It may be my Lord needs help.'

The girl looked beseechingly at him and put her hand on his arm as he turned away.

'No! Do not leave us! Do not cast us adrift for how would we find safety without you to guide us? We are lost...'

Durwyn cried as if to add his voice to the question.

The boy was still. Torn. The three people who now relied on him could not indeed be left. His shoulders sagged a little as he spoke.

'I shall only watch and see. No-one will see me and I will return ere long. Stay here until then.'

Giving the reins of his horse to the girl he turned away following the commotion.

The girl's sobs died in her throat. He would return. He could not now be lost not now that he had come back to her. For if he did not then she would die here. Even though Durwyn and the couple still needed her, her heart would finally give way. She knew this but reached for Durwyn and took him in her arms and buried her face in his curls, clutching his small body to her while his horse cropped contentedly at the short grass. The couple looked at her silently but with no reproach in their eyes. They trusted her. Durwyn slept.

CHAPTER FORTY-SEVEN

The boy slowed his step as the noise grew louder, and he could hear the cries of wounded and dying men. His hand fell to his sword but he was unwilling to involve himself yet. Although he had stood by his Lord's shoulder many times in fights and battles, yet now he thought he might be done with fighting at last. He sighed and his mind was filled with thoughts of the girl who waited.

CHAPTER FORTY-EIGHT

The Northman and the Outlaw fought back to back while the raven flew off to scream and berate all from the bough of a gnarled oak. The fighting was surprisingly fierce. The villagers had much to lose – the warrior band not so much. They were tiring.

'Enough!' shouted the Lord to his men. 'We must retreat to the ships! Now is not our time to die!'

And with that he wheeled round on his horse crashing towards the beach followed by his angry warriors who felt betrayed at being taken from the slaughter.

The Outlaw raced past him and hauled on the reins bringing the horse to a sudden halt, the raven flying behind him like paper blown by the wind, black and dark.

'Not our time to die?' he roared. 'I'll decide when that is, not you, you northern cur!'

He lifted his arm and knocked the warrior out of his saddle and without a backward glance he thundered back to the fray gathering uncertain warriors behind him so that at last the Lord was alone.

Sliding beneath his horse's feet he clutched his chest at the sudden pain and was unable to breathe. He was just able to make out the form of the boy who came creeping to him from out of the undergrowth.

'My Lord,' he said. 'You are hurt?' He felt for wounds. He looked for blood. There was none.

'You came back, my boy, you came back! I knew you would! That damned half-breed! I knew he was mistaken! I should have waited... But I hurt – oh, how I hurt!' And his face contorted in his agony.

The boy surprised himself by seeing tears fall on his hands as they lay on his Lord and was confused. He it had been who had destroyed his village, lost him his love and yet here he was weeping for the man who had always treated him kindly and with respect once he had earned it.

His Lord pulled him down and spoke softly, his breath dying away at the last.

'Go – and tell my daughter. Tell her that I am dead. Do not let her wait for me. Tell her I died with my sword in my hand and will dine this night in Valhalla with my ancestors and the gods. Go – and go safely…'

No more words came and his breath faded, finally. He grew still and silent.

For a moment the boy was unable to think. To know what to do. Then he laid his Lord down on the soft earth, closing his eyes and ensuring that his hands were gripping his sword so that the warrior maidens would know him and take him home.

He looked towards the clamour and uproar of a battle in which no quarter would be given or expected when a hoarse cry from above his head caused him to look up. The raven sat there hopping up and down on a branch above his head, peering down at him with malevolence in his eye. It flew off.

Suddenly the boy moved and tugging on his Lord's horse he moved off quickly back to what seemed to be now a new life. He smiled. They must move quickly.

CHAPTER FORTY-NINE

At the sound of horses the girl was afraid and made to run along with the couple and the baby, but there was a soft shout and a hissing which made her pause and listen carefully. A smile broke over her face and her eyes softened at the realisation that it was the boy come back to claim her and keep her safe.

And then he was there.

'Come, my Lord is dead and I have his horse. We will have need of it.'

The girl gave Durwyn back to his foster mother who found him a husk of bread on which to chew. She was helped onto the Viking's horse and though looked unsteady made no complaint. They were all beyond complaining. The girl mounted behind her. It was a sturdy little horse used to a warrior's bulk and weapons of iron. He too made no complaint.

The boy helped the man onto his own horse and preceding them on foot, led them towards the shore.

CHAPTER FIFTY

The Outlaw fought like a man possessed, denying any quarter or mercy until the villagers had all been destroyed. He leaned on his saddle gazing round at his weary men and those others who had fought as fiercely as they had, ignoring the wound that he had somehow acquired in the fighting which was beginning at last to hurt and he noticed the blood oozing from his sword arm which was cut about. He tore a strip from his clothes with his sword which he lashed around, staunching the flow immediately. He grunted and looked up. The fit and the wounded looked back at him on weary mounts whose heads hung quietly, too tired even to pick at the grass beneath their hooves.

All was quiet save for the flapping raven landing now on his master's shoulder. The Outlaw stroked his feathers.

'So you've come back, my bird, and what did you see I wonder?'

The raven was quiet and kept his own counsel.

'You Northmen – will you stay with me or will you go? I care not one way or the other. The choice is yours. But if you go – go now. I know not where your Lord is nor do I care,' he spat at the thought of him and his treachery.

The Northmen talked amongst themselves for some moments.

'We leave. We have helped you win your fight and will take whatever we can find as our reward. We will not return.'

They searched the bodies for aught of worth. The pickings were slim and took little time to collect.

'We will, I think, return to the boats and set sail for our home in the north. The air seems cleaner there.'

The speaker was a tall Viking with a piercing gaze. The Outlaw shrugged.

'Whatever you wish.'

And he inclined his head as he watched them go with not a little relief. He was happy to see them go. These Northmen were an unpredictable people. They made him uncomfortable.

He smiled as his raven sat comfortably on his shoulder and chattered softly in his ear. If only he was truly Odin's bird that flew through the Nine Worlds bringing back news of all that occurred there. Still, he loved his pet.

CHAPTER FIFTY-ONE

The weary band of travellers stumbled through the forest as dusk turned to night. Durwyn was hungry and grizzling. A nest was made for him on the forest floor and a piece of bread torn from their dwindling stores. He quieted and was content. A small stream ran nearby and the cool water was welcome.

The horses were hobbled and let loose to find what fodder they could, and rest.

The boy sat then with his back against a large tree and allowed himself to relax though not yet sleep. Too many thoughts and questions were rolling through his head. He looked at the girl through half-closed eyes and watched her make the couple as comfortable as she was able before settling herself onto the forest floor by Durwyn should he wake and need her. He needed her. But now was not the time.

He sighed.

She looked at the boy hardly believing what her own eyes were telling her. For so long he had been dead to her and was now returned. Her mind was in turmoil and she was glad of the darkness which hid her face from him. She did not think that sleep would come quickly, but in this she was mistaken for no sooner had her head rested on her arm than her heavy eyelids closed and a sigh escaped her lips.

The couple lay quiet and fearful. Sleep would not come to them. They whispered and wondered together what might become of them all. Yet they had little choice but to follow this strange pair who of a sudden were so filled with the thought of each other that they seemed apart from the world and strange as if touched by the gods.

Night wore on and all slept with nothing to disturb them until the first call of the blackbirds brought on the dawn and the horses could be heard in the stream.

The boy woke first and stretched waiting for his head to clear and the memories of yesterday to filter through the haze of sleep. As he moved towards the stream the others too left their resting places. Durwyn was lying waving his little arms in the air and gurgling to himself. The woman picked him up and gave him water. He drank eagerly and laughed as drops of water ran down his chin and he grabbed for the bread that was held out to him.

The horses were fetched and made ready. The girl helped and was quite alarmed at how she felt when her fingers accidentally touched his as they struggled with buckles and packs. She hoped her face did not betray her and wondered if he felt the same.

'Today we will reach the shoreline, I think,' said the boy, trying to ignore the feelings in his fingers that touched hers also. 'Then we will be safe.'

The woman and the man arranged themselves on the horses with the baby whilst the girl walked alongside the boy holding the reins of each horse.

Neither spoke for after all, what was there to say to each other?

Everything and nothing.

CHAPTER FIFTY-TWO

It seemed to be a long day though no-one complained and Durwyn seemed to find the rhythmic movement of the horse soothing and comfortable. They stopped to eat and rest the horses, and continued on their way.

As the afternoon drew on the boy could finally hear the sound of the sea and when they left the shelter of the trees the shoreline spread out before them and all stopped to look. The couple had never seen such a sight and the girl too was startled at the immensity of the sea.

'I knew naught of the sea. I never ventured this far from my village. I knew that this was the Whale Road on which the Northmen travelled but little else. It is beautiful.'

They stood gazing in awe at the immensity of sky

and sea which was quiet and calm and filled the boy with hope.

He turned them left and they walked carefully over the shingle dotted with sea wrack and driftwood. The boy was glad to see the driftwood. It would burn well.

As they rounded a small headland the boy grew anxious and searched restlessly for the place where he had been nursed and brought back to life. Perhaps it would no longer be there. Had been claimed by the sea and its storms. Or merely decayed.

And then he could see the little hut much worn but standing, still. He knew that his nurse would no longer inhabit the little hovel but he hoped that it would provide rest and a hiding place at last, until times were safer and kinder.

'We will be safe here. I was kept safe here and it has memories of comfort and care for me. It will care for you all I think, as well.' And smiling, he left his horse to push open the little door and enter.

It was with relief that the couple slid off their mounts standing a little unsteadily but glad to be back on their own feet. The girl held the horses while the boy pushed open the little gate and moved inside.

His eyes quickly became used to the gloom and he could make out the grey ashes of long-dead fires and a rusty pot hanging over them. The little wooden cot on which he had screamed and slept and almost died was still there though the rags under which he had sweated had long since turned to dust.

He turned at the sound of breathing behind him. The girl was there and he felt himself dizzy with longing. Reaching out to touch her hair as if to reassure himself that she was indeed real he held his breath and then he breathed again as she leaned into him and his arms went around her and they clutched each other silently for moments that seemed to encompass lifetimes.

The couple came through the door and Durwyn cried out in alarm at the darkness though the boy and girl saw only light. They stood apart but their fingers touched as if frightened to let go.

The woman smiled.

'We can live here. We can make a home for Durwyn as well. There is much to do.' And she moved around the small room, picking up things and moving things. Arranging in her head what needed to be done first.

'I will find wood. I noticed it on the shore and will gather as much as I am able. All will be well.' And the man turned such a look of kindliness on the girl and the boy that they felt blessed.

The boy followed him out and showed him where it had been piled up when he was here last, in a sheltered corner to keep dry. The man nodded and went down the overgrown path.

CHAPTER FIFTY-THREE

Before day's end there was a fire going in the cleaned-out hearth and a pot was boiling above it. The little home was becoming warmer as it became lived in and holes had been hastily patched to keep out the sea breezes. Durwyn was snug in a basket that they had found under rags. The darker corners would be left for the next day.

The boy wondered about the woman who had nursed him. Would he find her or at least her remains? He rather hoped so. He would take care of her. He owed her so much.

Somehow there was warm food for them all and though meagre it was warm and all were thankful for it.

'I'll set traps tomorrow – see if I can catch some coneys. I don't think I have forgotten how to.' And the man laughed.

'I can show you how to fish,' said the boy. 'And how to smoke and salt so you are able to store up provisions for the winter months.'

'Will you not be here?' asked the girl in some distress. She thought that they might always stay there together but seemingly it wasn't to be.

'I have a promise to keep. I must return to the north for a short time but I will return as soon as I am able. Stay here so I shall know where to find you. I mustn't lose you again.'

'But how will you travel there? How much longer must I wait? It has been a lifetime already…' And her voice faded with sadness.

'I will find a boat going north. There are many little boats – I saw them on my voyage down. There may be even a longboat on which I could make myself useful. And then I will return.'

'And what is this promise? A promise that is more important than us? I don't understand.'

'I promised my Lord that I would tell his daughter of his death. I must do this – it is a promise and oath-breakers are cursed. Forgive me.'

And the girl was desolate as she thought of all that

she had endured since last she saw him. How could she let him go? How would she be able to watch him walk away from her? But she knew she must and that she must not try and stop him. So, gathering herself together she stood and took his hand. They walked out into the forest.

The man and the woman were silent, grieving for the pair of them, knowing how slim were the chances of him returning. How dangerous were all Vikings. They covered the fire, tucked and soothed Durwyn who was almost asleep by now, warm and fed, and found themselves a place to sleep.

CHAPTER FIFTY-FOUR

The night was warm and filled with starlight.

They moved to the edge of the trees and sat on soft grass with the wide, wide sea in front of them. They were silent and then as one they turned to each other and clung together like people drowning in a flood.

This was no time for tears or any time beyond what they had at this moment.

Hands reached out, stroking and caressing and shivers ran through them both as they stretched out touching along the length of them. And slowly, slowly they came together in a tumble of cast-aside clothes feeling no cold, no discomfort, no shame but only love.

The boy noticed that she was no longer a girl and he was certainly no longer a boy. The girl felt scars on his body and ran her fingers down tracks whether left by knife or sword she knew not.

A gibbous moon hung above the sea silvering their skin as it moved across the sky casting shadows into the hollows of their bodies. It shone in the eyes of the girl as she looked into the eyes and heart of the boy and thought that she might drown. And she was glad to.

CHAPTER FIFTY-FIVE

The morning was bright and clear. Durwyn was awake and chuckling to himself and waving his little fists in the air. The woman rose to see to him and saw the girl open her eyes.

'We shall need more to eat soon especially for the child. My husband will have to go find a village which may let us have food.'

'I know,' said the girl. 'There is much to do before this becomes our home.'

The woman was quiet while she thought.

'I do not think that this can be our home for long. We need to find shelter elsewhere, I think, so that there will be people.'

The girl said naught for the woman was right and she was dismayed.

The boy came into the gloom of the little hut with dry kindling and wood and he set about making a fire amongst the cold ashes of long-ago fires. At last there was a small flame which gradually grew stronger and helped dispel the shadows which still clung to the corners. The man came through the door carrying a pot of water which the woman took and put to boil on the fire. The boy stood in the doorway and was silent. All eyes were drawn to him and even Durwyn was still.

He took a deep breath and spoke softly.

'I have tethered the horses close by so they won't wander. I will leave one when I go so you may use him or trade him. He is a good horse and has been with me since a colt. I will take my Lord's steed.'

The girl was mute and felt her blood run cold at the thought of losing him again so soon. The boy turned to her.

'I will head north tomorrow. I shall make for the river where it meets the sea. There will be men going north and I shall go with them. I have to go. I am under an obligation. But I will return and I will claim you as my bride, finally.'

And he reached out his hands and took her cold ones in his, rubbing her fingers warm. But she thought she might never be warm again if he left her.

CHAPTER FIFTY-SIX

The man and the boy took the horse and went in search of a settlement or a village where they could find the necessities needed to make their life by the sea more comfortable.

As they walked into the trees the boy was careful to watch and listen in case there were others about, whose intentions might not be peaceful. He was tired of fighting and besides, he had left his sword behind. The girl had charge of it and he knew, would wield it well should the need arise. But he didn't think she would need its protection now. They were safe. He was sure.

They came across a steading in a clearing and hailed the man working there in the warm earth. They spoke for some time and left with fresh bread, oats and the promise of a goat if they returned a week hence.

The farmer told them of a village close by. There had been no fighting or trouble of any kind in many years. It was quite a way from the sea and this might have been the reason that it had been left alone by raiders. It might be possible to live there perhaps. The man looked hopeful. He and his wife preferred living alongside others. The boy was evasive and left the man there tending his vegetables.

Returning to their refuge they found that the sun had come out and was lighting up the little hut and it looked welcoming. The boy knew that the girl would be safe here and was glad.

The woman was pleased to hear of the goat. Durwyn needed milk. The bread was quickly divided up and devoured. They were all hungry still.

CHAPTER FIFTY-SEVEN

The boy and the girl spent the day together walking along the seashore, sitting on the mossy rocks. The couple left them alone. There was nothing they could say to alter things, to make things better, and they were sad for the young couple.

Much was said that day on the rocks by the sea and by evening the girl was exhausted and hurting and wanted only to sleep. She turned to her sleeping place. The boy put out his hand to stay her but let it fall to his side after all. What could he do or say to make her feel less desolate?

CHAPTER FIFTY-EIGHT

Early in the morning as a pale sun rose above the horizon the boy gathered together what he thought he might need. With a heavy heart he loaded up his horse which was restive, wanting to be away. There was no movement from inside the little home already feeling warm and welcoming as the occupants worked to clean and clear and mend.

He slowed down his preparations hoping that she would come out at the last.

But it wasn't to be.

He mounted his horse and moved off, turning its head to the north and keeping to the edge of the shingle whilst his thoughts dwelt ceaselessly on the girl until he could bear it no longer and kicked his surprised horse into a gallop, letting the wind whip his hair and cause tears to spring to his eyes.

CHAPTER FIFTY-NINE

She heard him go and thought her heart would break completely and finally. But still she breathed and still she moved and the sun still rose higher in the sky through the morning.

The woman brought her broth and made her drink. She sat with her as her husband played with Durwyn and kept him busy and quiet.

And then as evening drew on sobs began to rack her body and she convulsed with pain and grief.

The woman covered her and stroked her hair until she fell asleep with exhaustion. Then she and her husband discussed what they might do when the girl realised that they could not stay here with the baby.

They rather thought that they would like to be a part of the village that the man had heard about.

There would be friends for Durwyn and no-one need know that he was a chief's son. His life would be that of a farmer and would be therefore quiet and away from strife.

At this thought, they were quiet, hoping that it would indeed be away from strife.

The couple had no idea what had become of their village or their chief and were content thinking that they were safe.

CHAPTER SIXTY

Days passed slowly and the little family in the safety of the old hut went about the tasks necessary for their survival and continuing comfort. The man caught fish in the surf and managed to trap and skin a coney. He showed the girl how to do this and how to cure the skin so that she would be warm when the cold came.

The girl though wan and pale and always quiet, spent her time with Durwyn. He was truly a lovely child and brought her heart a little ease.

The man returned with a goat after a foray to the steading, and fresh bread and oats. He spoke.

'We can go to the village, the farmer said. There is room for us all there and we would be welcome. I think we should go as soon as we may.'

The woman looked pleased but the girl shook her head.

'I can't join you. I must stay here so that he will know where to find me when he returns to me.' She smiled. 'He will return. He promised.'

And with that refused to say any more about leaving.

Although the couple were upset and worried about her decision they did not bother her with their protestations but made ready to leave.

'We will leave you the goat. She will be company for you and she can be milked for some time yet. I will visit and bring you news of Durwyn and also replenish your oats and perhaps help with planting so that you will have crops to store for the winter.'

'Thank you – both of you. I am glad that you will be safe and settled. I will come to see Durwyn. His smile has helped me to live when I thought that I might never smile again and would not live to see him grow up. I am pleased that you will be taking the horse with you. A horse will be most useful in your new life and I shall not need him. I will not be going anywhere.'

And she smiled and was silent, standing at the door as the couple and the little boy left her there, alone.

And so the pattern of her days was set.

Each morning she would go to the shore, raking the horizon with eyes tired from searching for any sign of the boy's return.

And so the days wore on.

CHAPTER SIXTY-ONE

After following the shoreline and staying out of sight under the trees for some days, the boy at last found a fishing vessel drawn up on the strand near to a small huddle of huts which was almost a village. He spoke to the men there who were coiling ropes and stowing supplies. They would be sailing north within the next day or so, happy to take him with them. Another strong man was always welcome.

He sold his horse to the headman who had come down to the boat with bread for the fisherman. He was loath to leave the beast but he had to travel north as fast as he may and he could not take him in this small boat. Another horse wold be bought when the need arose. He would fulfil his oath and return south.

Sailing close to the shore, the boat limped around each headland fighting headwinds and turbulent seas.

The fishermen had scant reward for their efforts with hook and line and had little to trade with the villages when they put in for fresh water but still they moved northwards. The boy's eyes were turned ever in that direction as if the intensity of his gaze could end his journey more quickly.

And time seemed slow and endless.

CHAPTER SIXTY-TWO

Until finally the wind turned them into a river mouth busy with craft of many shapes and the little boat pulled up at a wharf and was tied safely.

Gathering his few belongings the boy bid farewell and made his way through the noisy throng looking for familiar faces. None of those with whom he sailed south had returned and he spent fruitless hours searching for some evidence of his former life. It seemed that his Lord's people had left their encampment by the wharves. News of his death had obviously preceded his arrival and the boy was nonplussed.

That night he found a place to sleep out of the wind and arranged his things so that they would not be disturbed. He found a brew house close by and sat down on a stool near the fire and waited.

Men came and went and then the boy was stunned to see the Outlaw swagger past. There were two ravens on his shoulders this time and he was laughing with his warriors.

The boy sank back into the shadows and was hidden.

A fisherman paused with his drink halfway to his mouth and looked at him thoughtfully.

'The half-breed bastard frightens you, eh? And so he should.' He spat into the embers of the fire at his feet. 'See the ravens? He carries two now though once he had only the one. He took the other when he brought news of its master's death to his daughter.' He paused. 'He wasn't kind.'

The boy was quiet, thoughts churning in his head.

'Where is his daughter? I had hoped to see her and bring news of her father.'

The man looked at him through half-closed eyes.

'You sailed with him?'

'I did. And I was there at his dying. I made a promise to him and he went to his gods more easily but now I fear I may never find his daughter.'

'I think that you may find them up on the hillside above. They left some days ago. Though I know not how long they may be there and the number who left weren't many. It seems that bastard with the birds offered places in his band and men there were who took him up on his offer.' He spat again and was silent for a while. 'Men are fickle creatures and many have short memories. They proved themselves worthless in the end.'

The boy gazed out into the darkness beyond the glow of the dying fire.

'I must find them – speak to my Lord's daughter. And then I can return to fulfil my own destiny.'

His face was transcended with a kind of searing joy at the thought of the girl waiting on that long, grey shoreline. The fisherman looked at him with kindness. He was an old man now but he could remember what it felt like to love and be loved.

'It is late now and you need to rest. And I need to return to my bed also.' The fisherman rose at last and clasped his shoulder. 'I wish you well and may the goddess Freyja hold you in her arms.'

And with that the two men rose and left the brew house and the fire was doused and all was dark.

CHAPTER SIXTY-THREE

The following day the boy rose early and packed his things with a hopeful heart. Perhaps by the end of this day he may turn his face southwards forever.

He crossed over the river and turned his face towards the looming hulk of the ancient abbey above him on the hill, and pressed on.

Reaching the top of the hill he turned away from the abbey, making for the road that passed it by. He was sure that this would lead him to the place where his Lord's family dwelt after what the fisherman had told him. He paused, gathering himself, and was about to move on when behind him he heard a commotion and above him were the cries of birds. He looked up to see two ravens flying close by him.

He turned to find the Outlaw sauntering along the

road with several of his men and his soul was dismayed. The Outlaw shouted.

'So – I find the traitor who left us in the forest to be cut down by his friends.' He flicked his hand dismissively. 'They did not. We were victorious.' And he grinned viciously.

The boy was rooted to the spot and knew that his death was upon him.

As he stood and watched, the Outlaw closed the distance between them and stopped.

The boy stood his ground and would not show fear in his last moments, standing straight and staring into the Outlaw's dead eyes.

The bringer of death raised his arm and the boy saw the bright sword arc through the clean air. He followed it with his eyes, the eyes of a man staring at the destiny which now drew him on.

He thought of the girl left waiting forever. His last thoughts were of her, her eyes gazing at him with love, as the darkness descended and he fell, with his shield broken and the life bleeding out of him.

The ravens settled on his body, attracted by the smell of blood, and began to feed. The Outlaw watched for a moment then turned away, leaving his birds to their feast.

The birds flapped their great wings and followed their master.

The hill was quiet and the world turned and the bones of the boy whitened through the seasons.

CHAPTER SIXTY-FOUR

The boy Durwyn grew and came to care for the girl over the years and would bring news.

Warriors ceased fighting and settled in ruined villages, returning life to them and making them live once more.

The land was quiet.

And the girl turned at the last into an old woman.

EPILOGUE

And so I shall live out my days on this long, grey shoreline, ever gazing and searching for that which is no longer there. And I will weep – weep for what has gone and will never be more. And I will grow old and my clothes will become rags and my hair will fade, and my eyes will dim as I become an old woman at last. But I will see all with my heart and the inner eye which is ever clear. And one day I shall at last fly with the ravens and drift on the wind and only then shall I leave this place, desolate and deserted and there will be

Silence

And Peace…

ABOUT THE AUTHOR

Jane Corton lives with her husband Mick and miniature schnauzer, in a little mill village on the edge of the Pennines.

A retired Year 3 teacher, she spends her time pootling in the garden, painting, and reading – lots of reading.

Raven's Cry is her first published story.

35072597R00132

Printed in Poland
by Amazon Fulfillment
Poland Sp. z o.o., Wrocław